John Pinkerton, Abel Janszoon Tasman, William Dampier

Early Australian Voyages

Pelsart, Tasman, Dampier

John Pinkerton, Abel Janszoon Tasman, William Dampier

Early Australian Voyages
Pelsart, Tasman, Dampier

ISBN/EAN: 9783337313807

Printed in Europe, USA, Canada, Australia, Japan

Cover: Foto ©Andreas Hilbeck / pixelio.de

More available books at **www.hansebooks.com**

CASSELL'S NATIONAL LIBRARY

EARLY
AUSTRALIAN VOYAGES

𝔓𝔢𝔩𝔰𝔞𝔯𝔱   𝔗𝔞𝔰𝔪𝔞𝔫   𝔇𝔞𝔪𝔭𝔦𝔢𝔯

BY

JOHN PINKERTON

CASSELL & COMPANY Limited

LONDON PARIS & MELBOURNE

1893

INTRODUCTION.

In the days of Plato, imagination found its way, before the mariners, to a new world across the Atlantic, and fabled an Atlantis where America now stands. In the days of Francis Bacon, imagination of the English found its way to the great Southern Continent before the Portuguese or Dutch sailors had sight of it, and it was the home of those wise students of God and nature to whom Bacon gave his New Atlantis. The discoveries of America date from the close of the fifteenth century. The discoveries of Australia date only from the beginning of the seventeenth. The discoveries of the Dutch were little known in England before the time of Dampier's voyage, at the close of the seventeenth century, with which this volume ends. The name of New Holland, first given by the Dutch to the land they discovered on the north-west coast, then extended to the continent and was since changed to Australia.

During the eighteenth century exploration was continued by the English. The good report of Captain Cook caused the first British settlement to be made at Port Jackson, in 1788, not quite a hundred years ago, and the foundations were then laid of the settlement of New South Wales, or Sydney. It was at first a penal colony, and its Botany Bay was a name of terror to offenders. Western Australia, or Swan River, was first settled as a free colony in 1829, but afterwards used also as a penal settlement; South Australia, which has Adelaide for its capital, was first established in 1834, and colonised in 1836; Victoria, with Melbourne for its capital, known until 1851 as the Port Philip District, and a dependency of New South Wales, was first colonised in 1835. It received in 1851 its present name. Queensland, formerly known as the Moreton Bay District, was established as late as 1859. A settlement of North Australia was tried in 1838, and has since been abandoned. On the other side of Bass's Straits, the island of Van Diemen's Land, was named Tasmania, and established as a penal colony in 1803.

Advance, Australia! The scattered handfuls of people have become a nation, one with us in race, and character, and worthiness of aim. These little volumes will, in course of time, include many aids to a knowledge of the shaping of the nations. There will be later records of Australia than those which tell of the old Dutch explorers, and of the first real awakening of England to a knowledge of Australia by Dampier's voyage.

The great Australian continent is 2,500 miles long from east to west, and 1,960 miles in its greatest breadth. Its climates are therefore various. The northern half lies chiefly within the tropics, and at Melbourne snow is seldom seen except upon the hills. The separation of Australia by wide seas from Europe, Asia, Africa, and America, gives it animals and plants peculiarly its own. It has been said that of 5,710 plants discovered, 5,440 are peculiar to that continent. The kangaroo also is proper to Australia, and there are other animals of like kind. Of 58 species of quadruped found in Australia, 46 were peculiar to it. Sheep and cattle that abound there now were introduced from Europe. From eight merino sheep introduced in 1793 by a settler named McArthur, there has been multiplication into millions, and the food-store of the Old World begins to be replenished by Australian mutton.

The unexplored interior has given a happy hunting-ground to satisfy the British spirit of adventure and research; but large waterless tracts, that baffle man's ingenuity, have put man's powers of endurance to sore trial.

The mountains of Australia are all of the oldest rocks, in which there are either no fossil traces of past life, or the traces are of life in the most ancient forms. Resemblance of the Australian cordilleras to the Ural range, which he had especially been studying, caused Sir Roderick Murchison, in 1844, to predict that gold would be found in Australia. The first finding of gold —the beginning of the history of the Australian gold-fields — was in February, 1851, near Bathurst and Wellington, and to-day looks back to the morning of yesterday in the name of Ophir, given to the Bathurst gold-diggings.

Gold, wool, mutton, wine, fruits, and what more Australia can now add to the commonwealth of the English-speaking people, Englishmen at home have been learning this year in the great Indian and Colonial Exhibition, which is to stand always as evidence of the numerous resources of the Empire, as aid to the full knowledge of them, and through that to their wide diffusion. We are a long way now from the wrecked ship of Captain Francis Pelsart, with which the histories in this volume begin.

John Pinkerton was born at Edinburgh in February, 1758, and died in Paris in March, 1826, aged sixty-eight. He was the best classical scholar at the Lanark grammar school; but his father, refusing to send him to a university, bound him to Scottish law. He had a strong will, fortified in some respects by a weak judgment. He wrote clever verse; at the age of twenty-two he went to London to support himself by literature, began by publishing "Rimes" of his own, and then Scottish Ballads, all issued as ancient, but of which he afterwards admitted that fourteen out of the seventy-three were wholly written by himself. John Pinkerton, whom Sir Walter Scott described as "a man of considerable learning, and some severity as well as acuteness of disposition," made clear conscience on the matter in 1786, when he published two volumes of genuine old Scottish Poems from the MS. collections of Sir Richard Maitland. He had added to his credit as an antiquary by an Essay on Medals, and then applied his studies to ancient Scottish History, producing learned books, in which he bitterly abused the Celts. It was in 1802 that Pinkerton left England for Paris, where he supported himself by indefatigable industry as a writer during the last twenty-four years of his life. One of the most useful of his many works was that *General Collection of the best and most interesting Voyages and Travels of the World*, which appeared in seventeen quarto volumes, with maps and engravings, in the years 1808—1814. Pinkerton abridged and digested most of the travellers' records given in this series, but always studied to retain the travellers' own words, and his occasional comments have a value of their own.

H. M.

EARLY AUSTRALIAN VOYAGES.

VOYAGE OF FRANCIS PELSART TO AUSTRALASIA.

1628 — 29.

IT has appeared very strange to some very able judges of voyages, that the Dutch should make so great account of the southern countries as to cause the map of them to be laid down in the pavement of the Stadt House at Amsterdam, and yet publish no descriptions of them. This mystery was a good deal heightened by one of the ships that first touched on Carpenter's Land, bringing home a considerable quantity of gold, spices, and other rich goods ; in order to clear up which, it was said that these were not the product of the country, but were fished out of the wreck of a large ship that had been lost upon the coast. But this story did not satisfy the inquisitive, because not attended with circumstances necessary to establish its credit ; and therefore they suggested that, instead of taking away the obscurity by relating the truth, this story was invented in order to hide it more effectually. This suspicion gained ground the

more when it was known that the Dutch East India
Company from Batavia had made some attempts to
conquer a part of the Southern continent, and had
been repulsed with loss, of which, however, we have
no distinct or perfect relation, and all that hath
hitherto been collected in reference to this subject,
may be reduced to two voyages, All that we know
concerning the following piece is, that it was collected
from the Dutch journal of the voyage, and having
said thus much by way of introduction, we now proceed to the translation of this short history.

The directors of the East India Company, animated
by the return of five ships, under General Carpenter,
richly laden, caused, the very same year, 1628, eleven
vessels to be equipped for the same voyage; amongst
which there was one ship called the *Batavia*, commanded by Captain Francis Pelsart. They sailed out
of the Texel on the 28th of October, 1628; and as it
would be tedious and troublesome to the reader to set
down a long account of things perfectly well known, I
shall say nothing of the occurrences that happened in
their passage to the Cape of Good Hope; but content
myself with observing that on the 4th of June, in the
following year 1629, this vessel, the *Batavia*, being
separated from the fleet in a storm, was driven on the
Abrollos or shoals, which lie in the latitude of 28 degrees
south, and which have been since called by the Dutch,
the Abrollos of Frederic Houtman. Captain Pelsart,
who was sick in bed when this accident happened, per-

ceiving that his ship had struck, ran immediately upon deck. It was night indeed; but the weather was fair, and the moon shone very bright; the sails were up; the course they steered was north-east by north, and the sea appeared as far as they could behold it covered with a white froth. The captain called up the master and charged him with the loss of the ship, who excused himself by saying he had taken all the care he could; and that having discerned this froth at a distance, he asked the steersman what he thought of it, who told him that the sea appeared white by its reflecting the rays of the moon. The captain then asked him what was to be done, and in what part of the world he thought they were. The master replied, that God only knew that; and that the ship was fast on a bank hitherto undiscovered. Upon this they began to throw the lead, and found that they had forty-eight feet of water before, and much less behind the vessel. The crew immediately agreed to throw their cannon overboard, in hopes that when the ship was lightened she might be brought to float again. They let fall an anchor however; and while they were thus employed, a most dreadful storm arose of wind and rain; which soon convinced them of the danger they were in; for being surrounded with rocks and shoals, the ship was continually striking.

They then resolved to cut away the main-mast, which they did, and this augmented the shock, neither could they get clear of it, though they cut it close by the board, because it was much entangled with the rigging ; they could see no land except an island which was about the distance of three leagues, and two smaller islands, or rather rocks, which lay nearer. They immediately sent the master to examine them, who returned about nine in the morning, and reported that the sea at high water did not cover them, but that the coast was so rocky and full of shoals that it would be very difficult to land upon them ; they resolved, however, to run the risk, and to send most of their company on shore to pacify the women, children, sick people, and such as were out of their wits with fear, whose cries and noise served only to disturb them. About ten o'clock they embarked these in their shallop and skiff, and, perceiving their vessel began to break, they doubled their diligence ; they likewise endeavoured to get their bread up, but they did not take the same care of the water, not reflecting in their fright that they might be much distressed for want of it on shore ; and what hindered them most of all was the brutal behaviour of some of the crew that made themselves drunk with wine, of which no care was taken. In short, such was their confusion that they made but three trips that day, carrying over to the island 180 persons, twenty barrels of bread, and some small casks of water. The master returned on board towards evening, and told the captain that it was to no purpose to send more provisions on shore, since the people only wasted those they had already. Upon this the captain went in the shallop,

to put things in better order, and was then informed
that there was no water to be found upon the island;
he endeavoured to return to the ship in order to bring
off a supply, together with the most valuable part
of their cargo, but a storm suddenly arising, he was
forced to return.

The next day was spent in removing their water
and most valuable goods on shore; and afterwards
the captain in the skiff, and the master in the shallop,
endeavoured to return to the vessel, but found the sea
run so high that it was impossible to get on board.
In this extremity the carpenter threw himself out of
the ship, and swam to them, in order to inform them
to what hardships those left in the vessel were reduced,
and they sent him back with orders for them to make
rafts, by tying the planks together, and endeavour on
these to reach the shallop and skiff; but before this
could be done, the weather became so rough that the
captain was obliged to return, leaving, with the utmost
grief, his lieutenant and seventy men on the very
point of perishing on board the vessel. Those who
were got on the little island were not in a much better
condition, for, upon taking an account of their water,
they found they had not above 40 gallons for 40
people, and on the larger island, where there were
120, their stock was still less. Those on the little
island began to murmur, and to complain of their
officers, because they did not go in search of water, in
the islands that were within sight of them, and they

represented the necessity of this to Captain **Pelsart**, who agreed to their request, but insisted before he went to communicate his design to the rest of the people; they consented to this, but not till the captain had declared that, without the consent of the company on the large island, he would, rather than leave them, go and perish on board the ship. When they were got pretty near the shore, he who commanded the boat told the captain that if he had anything to say, he must cry out to the people, for that they would not suffer him to go out of the boat. The captain immediately attempted to throw himself overboard in order to swim to the island. Those who were in the boat prevented him; and all that he could obtain from them was, to throw on shore his table-book, in which he wrote a line or two to inform them that he was gone in the skiff to look for water in the adjacent islands.

He accordingly coasted them all with the greatest care, and found in most of them considerable quantities of water in the holes of the rocks, but so mixed with the sea-water that it was unfit for use; and therefore they were obliged to go farther. The first thing they did was to make a deck to their boat, because they found it was impracticable to navigate those seas in an open vessel. Some of the crew joined them by the time the work was finished; and the captain having obtained a paper, signed by all his men, importing that it was their desire that he should go in search of water, he immediately put to sea, having first taken an observation by which he found they were in the latitude of 28 degrees 13 minutes south. They had not been long at sea before they had sight of the continent, which appeared to them to lie about sixteen miles north by west from the place they had suffered shipwreck. They found about twenty-five or thirty fathoms water; and as night drew on, they kept out to sea; and after midnight stood in for the land, that they might be near the coast in the morning. On the 9th of June they found themselves as they reckoned, about three miles from the shore; on which they plied all that day, sailing sometimes north, sometimes west; the country appearing low, naked, and the coast excessively rocky; so that they thought it resembled the country near Dover. At last they saw a little creek, into which they were willing to put, because it appeared to have a sandy bottom; but when they attempted to enter it, the sea ran so high that they were forced to desist.

On the 10th they remained on the same coast, plying to and again, as they had done the day before; but the weather growing worse and worse, they were obliged to abandon their shallop, and even throw part of their bread overboard, because it hindered them from clearing themselves of the water, which their vessel began to make very fast. That night it rained most terribly, which, though it gave them much trouble, afforded them hopes that it would prove a great relief to the people they had left behind them on the islands. The wind began to sink on the 11th; and as it blew from the west-south-west, they continued their course to the north, the sea running still so high that it was impossible to approach the shore. On the 12th, they had an observation, by which they found themselves in the latitude of 27 degrees; they sailed with a south-east wind all that day along the coast, which they found so steep that there was no getting on shore, inasmuch as there was no creek or low land without the rocks, as is commonly observed on sea-coasts; which gave them the more pain because within land the country appeared very fruitful and pleasant. They found themselves on the 13th in the latitude of 25 degrees 40 minutes; by which they discovered that the current set to the north. They were at this time over against an opening; the coast lying to the north-east, they continued a north course, but found the coast one continued rock of red colour all of a height, against which the waves broke with such force that it was impossible for them to land.

The wind blew very fresh in the morning on the 14th, but towards noon it fell calm; they were then in the height of 24 degrees, with a small gale at east, but the tide still carried them further north than they desired, because their design was to make a descent as soon as possible; and with this view they sailed slowly along the coast, till, perceiving a great deal of smoke at a distance, they rowed towards it as fast as they were able, in hopes of finding men, and water, of course. When they came near the shore, they found it so steep, so full of rocks, and the sea beating over them with such fury, that it was impossible to land. Six of the men, however, trusting to their skill in swimming, threw themselves into the sea and resolved to get on shore at any rate, which with great difficulty and danger they at last effected, the boat remaining at anchor in twenty-five fathoms water. The men on shore spent the whole day in looking for water; and while they were thus employed, they saw four men, who came up very near; but one of the Dutch sailors advancing towards them, they immediately ran away as fast as they were able, so that they were distinctly seen by those in the boat. These people were black savages, quite naked, not having so much as any covering about their middle. The sailors, finding no hopes of water on all the coast, swam on board again, much hurt and wounded by their being beat by the waves upon the rocks; and as soon as they were on board, they weighed anchor, and continued their course along the shore, in hopes of finding some better landing-place.

On the 25th, in the morning, they discovered a cape, from the point of which there ran a ridge of rocks a mile into the sea, and behind it another ridge of rocks. They ventured between them, as the sea was pretty calm; but finding there was no passage, they soon returned. About noon they saw another opening, and

the sea being still very smooth, they entered it, though
the passage was very dangerous, inasmuch as they had
but two feet water, and the bottom full of stones,
the coast appearing a flat sand for about a mile. As
soon as they got on shore] they fell to digging in the
sand, but the water that came into their wells was so
brackish that they could not drink it, though they
were on the very point of choking for thirst. At last,
in the hollows of the rocks, they met with considerable
quantities of rain-water, which was a great relief to
them, since they had been for some days at no better
allowance than a pint a-piece. They soon furnished
themselves in the night with about eighty gallons,
perceiving, in the place where they landed, that the
savages had been there lately, by a large heap of ashes
and the remains of some cray-fish.

On the 16th, in the morning, they returned on shore,
in hopes of getting more water, but were disappointed;
and having now time to observe the country, it gave
them no great hopes of better success, even if they had
travelled farther within land, which appeared a thirsty,
barren plain, covered with ant-hills, so high that they
looked afar off like the huts of negroes; and at the
same time they were plagued with flies, and those in
such multitudes that they were scarce able to defend
themselves. They saw at a distance eight savages,
with each a staff in his hand, who advanced towards
them within musket-shot; but as soon as they perceived the Dutch sailors moving towards them, they

fled as fast as they were able. It was by this time about noon, and, perceiving no appearance either of getting water, or entering into any correspondence with the natives, they resolved to go on board and continue their course towards the north, in hopes, as they were already in the latitude of 22 degrees 17 minutes, they might be able to find the river of Jacob Remmescens; but the wind veering about to the north-east, they were not able to continue longer upon that coast, and therefore reflecting that they were now above one hundred miles from the place where they were shipwrecked, and had scarce as much water as would serve them in their passage back, they came to a settled resolution of making the best of their way to Batavia, in order to acquaint the Governor-General with their misfortunes, and to obtain such assistance as was necessary to get their people off the coast.

On the 17th they continued their course to the north-east, with a good wind and fair weather; the 18th and 19th it blew hard, and they had much rain; on the 20th they found themselves in 19 degrees 22 minutes; on the 22nd they had another observation, and found themselves in the height of 16 degrees 10 minutes, which surprised them very much, and was a plain proof that the current carried them northwards at a great rate; on the 27th it rained very hard, so that they were not able to take an observation; but towards noon they saw, to their great satisfaction, the coasts of Java, in the latitude of 8 degrees, at the distance of about four or five miles. They altered their course to west-north-west, and towards evening entered the gulf of an island very full of trees, where they anchored in eight fathoms water, and there passed the night; on the 28th, in the morning, they weighed, and rowed with all their force, in order to make the land, that they might search for water, being now again at the point of perishing for thirst. Very happily for them, they were no sooner on shore than they discovered a fine rivulet at a small distance, where, having comfortably quenched their thirst, and filled all their casks with water, they about noon continued their course for Batavia.

On the 29th, about midnight, in the second watch, they discovered an island, which they left on their starboard. About noon they found themselves in the height of 6 degrees 48 minutes. About three in the afternoon they passed between two islands, the western-most of which appeared full of cocoa trees. In the evening they were about a mile from the south point of Java, and in the second watch exactly between Java and the Isle of Princes. The 30th, in the morning, they found themselves on the coast of the last-mentioned island, not being able to make above two miles that day. On July 1st the weather was calm, and about noon they were three leagues from Dwaersindenwegh, that is, Thwart-the-way Island; but towards the even-ing they had a pretty brisk wind at north-west, which enabled them to gain that coast. On the 2nd, in the

morning, they were right against the island of Topers-
hoetien, and were obliged to lie at anchor till eleven
o'clock, waiting for the sea-breeze, which, however,
blew so faintly that they were not able to make above
two miles that day. About sunset they perceived a
vessel between them and Thwart-the-way Island, upon
which they resolved to anchor as near the shore as they
could that night, and there wait the arrival of the ship.
In the morning they went on board her, in hopes of
procuring arms for their defence, in case the inhabitants
of Java were at war with the Dutch. They found two
other ships in company, on board one of which was
Mr. Ramburg, counsellor of the Indies. Captain
Pelsart went immediately on board his ship, where he
acquainted him with the nature of his misfortune, and
went with him afterwards to Batavia.

We will now leave the captain soliciting succours
from the Governor-General, in order to return to the
crew who were left upon the islands, among whom
there happened such transactions as, in their condition,
the reader would little expect, and perhaps will hardly
credit. In order to their being thoroughly understood,
it is necessary to observe that they had for supercargo
one Jerom Cornelis, who had been formerly an
apothecary at Harlem. This man, when they were on
the coast of Africa, had plotted with the pilot and
some others to run away with the vessel, and either to
carry her into Dunkirk, or to turn pirates in her on
their own account. This supercargo had remained ten

days on board the wreck, not being able in all that time to get on shore. Two whole days he spent on the mainmast, floating to and fro, till at last, by the help of one of the yards, he got to land. When he was once on shore, the command, in the absence of Captain Pelsart, devolved of course upon him, which immediately revived in his mind his old design, insomuch that he resolved to lay hold of this opportunity to make himself master of all that could be saved out of the wreck, conceiving that it would be easy to surprise the captain on his return, and determining to go on the account—that is to say, to turn pirate in the captain's vessel. In order to carry this design into execution, he thought necessary to rid themselves of such of the crew as were not like to come into their scheme; but before he proceeded to dip his hands in blood, he obliged all the conspirators to sign an instrument, by which they engaged to stand by each other.

The whole ship's company were on shore in three islands, the greatest part of them in that where Cornelis was, which island they thought fit to call the burying-place of Batavia. One Mr. Weybhays was sent with another body into an adjacent island to look for water, which, after twenty days' search, he found, and made the appointed signal by lighting three fires, which, however, were not seen nor taken notice of by those under the command of Cornelis, because they were busy in butchering their companions, of whom they had murdered between thirty and forty; but some

few, however, got off upon a raft of planks tied
together, and went to the island where Mr. Weybhays
was, in order to acquaint him with the dreadful
accident that had happened. Mr. Weybhays having
with him forty-five men, they all resolved to stand
upon their guard, and to defend themselves to the last
man, in case these villains should attack them. This
indeed was their design, for they were apprehensive
both of this body, and of those who were on the third
island, giving notice to the captain on his return, and
thereby preventing their intention of running away
with his vessel. But as this third company was by
much the weakest, they began with them first, and cut
them all off, except five women and seven children, not
in the least doubting that they should be able to do as
much by Weybhays and his company. In the meantime, having broke open the merchant's chests, which
had been saved out of the wreck, they converted them
to their own use without ceremony.

The traitor, Jerom Cornelis, was so much elevated
with the success that had hitherto attended his villainy,
that he immediately began to fancy all difficulties were
over, and gave a loose to his vicious inclinations in
every respect. He ordered clothes to be made of rich
stuffs that had been saved, for himself and his troop,
and having chosen out of them a company of guards,
he ordered them to have scarlet coats, with a double
lace of gold or silver. There were two minister's
daughters among the women, one of whom he took for

his own mistress, gave the second to a favourite of his, and ordered that the other three women should be common to the whole troop. He afterwards drew up a set of regulations, which were to be the laws of his new principality, taking to himself the style and title of Captain-General, and obliging his party to sign an act, or instrument, by which they acknowledged him as such. These points once settled, he resolved to carry on the war. He first of all embarked on board two shallops twenty-two men, well armed, with orders to destroy Mr. Weybhays and his company; and on their miscarrying, he undertook a like expedition with thirty-seven men, in which, however, he had no better success; for Mr. Weybhays, with his people, though armed only with staves with nails drove into their heads, advanced even into the water to meet them, and after a brisk engagement compelled these murderers to retire.

Cornelis then thought fit to enter into a negotiation, which was managed by the chaplain, who remained with Mr. Weybhays, and after several comings and goings from one party to the other, a treaty was concluded upon the following terms—viz., That Mr. Weybhays and his company should for the future remain undisturbed, provided they delivered up a little boat, in which one of the sailors had made his escape from the island in which Cornelis was with his gang, in order to take shelter on that where Weybhays was with his company. It was also agreed that the latter should have a part of the stuffs and silks given them for clothes, of which they stood in great want. But, while this affair was in agitation, Cornelis took the opportunity of the correspondence between them being restored, to write letters to some French soldiers that were in Weybhays's company, promising them six thousand livres apiece if they would comply with his demands, not doubting but by this artifice he should be able to accomplish his end.

His letters, however, had no effect; on the contrary, the soldiers to whom they were directed carried them immediately to Mr. Weybhays. Cornelis, not knowing that this piece of treachery was discovered, went over the next morning, with three or four of his people, to carry to Mr. Weybhays the clothes that had been promised him. As soon as they landed, Weybhays attacked them, killed two or three, and made Cornelis himself prisoner. One Wonterloss, who was the only man that made his escape, went immediately back to the conspirators, put himself at their head, and came the next day to attack Weybhays, but met with the same fate as before—that is to say, he and the villains that were with him were soundly beat.

Things were in this situation when Captain Pelsart arrived in the *Sardam* frigate. He sailed up to the wreck, and saw with great joy a cloud of smoke ascending from one of the islands, by which he knew that all his people were not dead. He came immediately to an anchor, and having ordered some wine and provisions

to be put into the skiff, resolved to go in person with
these refreshments to one of these islands. He had
hardly quitted the ship before he was boarded by a
boat from the island to which he was going. There
were four men in the boat, of whom Weybhays was
one, who immediately ran to the captain, told him what
had happened, and begged him to return to his ship
immediately, for that the conspirators intended to
surprise her, that they had already murdered 125
persons, and that they had attacked him and his
company that very morning with two shallops.

While they were talking the two shallops appeared;
upon which the captain rowed to his ship as fast as he
could, and was hardly got on board before they arrived
at the ship's side. The captain was surprised to see
men in red coats laced with gold and silver, with arms
in their hands. He demanded what they meant by
coming on board armed. They told him he should
know when they were on board the ship. The captain
replied that they should come on board, but that they
must first throw their arms into the sea, which if they
did not do immediately, he would sink them as they
lay. As they saw that disputes were to no purpose,
and that they were entirely in the captain's power,
they were obliged to obey. They accordingly threw
their arms overboard, and were then taken into the
vessel, where they were instantly put in irons. One
of them, whose name was John Bremen, and who was
first examined, owned that he had murdered with his

own hands, or had assisted in murdering, no less than twenty-seven persons. The same evening Weybhays brought his prisoner Cornelis on board, where he was put in irons and strictly guarded.

On the 18th of September, Captain Pelsart, with the master, went to take the rest of the conspirators in Cornelis's island. They went in two boats. The villains, as soon as they saw them land, lost all their courage, and fled from them. They surrendered without a blow, and were put in irons with the rest. The captain's first care was to recover the jewels which Cornelis had dispersed among his accomplices: they were, however, all of them soon found, except a gold chain and a diamond ring; the latter was also found at last, but the former could not be recovered. They went next to examine the wreck, which they found staved into an hundred pieces; the keel lay on a bank of sand on one side, the fore part of the vessel stuck fast on a rock, and the rest of her lay here and there as the pieces had been driven by the waves, so that Captain Pelsart had very little hopes of saving any of the merchandise. One of the people belonging to Weybhays's company told him that one fair day, which was the only one they had in a month, as he was fishing near the wreck, he had struck the pole in his hand against one of the chests of silver, which revived the captain a little, as it gave him reason to expect that something might still be saved. They spent all the 19th in examining the rest of the prisoners, and in confronting them with those who escaped from the massacre.

On the 20th they sent several kinds of refreshments to Weybhays's company, and carried a good quantity of water from the isle. There was something very singular in finding this water; the people who were on shore there had subsisted near three weeks on rain-water, and what lodged in the clefts of the rocks, without thinking that the water of two wells which were on the island could be of any use, because they saw them constantly rise and fall with the tide, from whence they fancied they had a communication with the sea, and consequently that the water must be brackish; but upon trial they found it to be very good, and so did the ship's company, who filled their casks with it.

On the 21st the tide was so low, and an east-south-east wind blew so hard, that during the whole day the boat could not get out. On the 22nd they attempted to fish upon the wreck, but the weather was so bad that even those who could swim very well durst not approach it. On the 25th the master and the pilot, the weather being fair, went off again to the wreck, and those who were left on shore, observing that they wanted hands to get anything out of her, sent off some to assist them. The captain went also himself to encourage the men, who soon weighed one chest of silver, and some time after another. As soon as these were safe ashore they returned to their work, but the

weather grew so bad that they were quickly obliged to
desist, though some of their divers from Guzarat
assured them they had found six more, which might
easily be weighed. On the 26th, in the afternoon, the
weather being fair, and the tide low, the master returned to the place where the chests lay, and weighed
three of them, leaving an anchor with a gun tied to it,
and a buoy, to mark the place where the fourth lay,
which, notwithstanding their utmost efforts, they were
not able to recover.

On the 27th the south wind blew very cold. On the
28th the same wind blew stronger than the day before;
and as there was no possibility of fishing in the wreck
for the present, Captain Pelsart held a council to consider what they should do with the prisoners: that is
to say, whether it would be best to try them there
upon the spot, or to carry them to Batavia, in order to
their being tried by the Company's officers. After
mature deliberation, reflecting on the number of
prisoners, and the temptation that might arise from
the vast quantity of silver on board the frigate, they
at last came to a resolution to try and execute them
there, which was accordingly done; and they embarked
immediately afterwards for Batavia.

REMARKS.

This voyage was translated from the original Dutch
by Thevenot, and printed by him in the first volume of

his collections. Pelsart's route is traced in the map of the globe published by Delisle in the year 1700.

As this voyage is of itself very short, I shall not detain the reader with many remarks; but shall confine myself to a very few observations, in order to show the consequences of the discovery made by Captain Pelsart. The country upon which he suffered shipwreck was New Holland, the coast of which had not till then been at all examined, and it was doubtful how far it extended. There had indeed been some reports spread with relation to the inhabitants of this country, which Captain Pelsart's relation shows to have been false; for it had been reported that when the Dutch East India Company sent some ships to make discoveries, their landing was opposed by a race of gigantic people, with whom the Dutch could by no means contend. But our author says nothing of the extraordinary size of the savages that were seen by Captain Pelsart's people; from whence it is reasonable to conclude that this story was circulated with no other view than to prevent other nations from venturing into these seas. It is also remarkable that this is the very coast surveyed by Captain Dampier, whose account agrees exactly with that contained in this voyage. Now though it be true, that from all these accounts there is nothing said which is much to the advantage either of the country or its inhabitants, yet we are to consider that it is impossible to represent either in a worse light than that in which the Cape of

Good Hope was placed, before the Dutch took possession of it; and plainly demonstrated that industry
could make a paradise of what was a perfect purgatory
while in the hands of the Hottentots. If, therefore, the
climate of this country bo good, and the soil fruitful,
both of which were affirmed in this relation, there
could not be a more proper place for a colony than
some part of New Holland, or of the adjacent country
of Carpentaria. I shall give my reasons for asserting
this when I come to make my remarks on a succeeding
voyage. At present I shall confine myself to the
reasons that have induced the Dutch East India Company to leave all these countries unsettled, after
having first shown so strong an inclination to discover
them, which will oblige me to lay before the reader
some secrets in commerce that have hitherto escaped
common observation, and which, whenever they are as
thoroughly considered as they deserve, will undoubtedly lead us to as great discoveries as those of
Columbus or Magellan.

In order to make myself perfectly understood, I must
observe that it was the finding out of the Moluccas, or
Spice Islands, by the Portuguese, that raised that spirit
of discovery which produced Columbus's voyage, which
ended in finding America; though in fact Columbus
intended rather to reach this country of New Holland.
The assertion is bold, and at first sight may appear
improbable; but a little attention will make it so plain,
that the reader must be convinced of the truth of what

I say. The proposition made by Columbus to the State of Genoa, the Kings of Portugal, Spain, England, and France, was this, that he could discover a new route to the East Indies; that is to say, without going round the Cape of Good Hope. He grounded this proposition on the spherical figure of the earth, from whence he thought it self-evident that any given point might be sailed to through the great ocean, either by steering east or west. In his attempt to go to the East Indies by a west course, he met with the islands and continent of America; and finding gold and other commodities, which till then had never been brought from the Indies, he really thought that this was the west coast of that country to which the Portuguese sailed by the Cape of Good Hope, and hence came the name of the West Indies. Magellan, who followed his steps, and was the only discoverer who reasoned systematically, and knew what he was doing, proposed to the Emperor Charles V. to complete what Columbus had begun, and to find a passage to the Moluccas by the west; which, to his immortal honour, he accomplished.

When the Dutch made their first voyages to the East Indies, which was not many years before Captain Pelsart's shipwreck on the coast of New Holland, for their first fleet arrived in the East Indies in 1596, and Pelsart lost his ship in 1629—I say, when the Dutch first undertook the East India trade, they had the Spice Islands in view; and as they are a nation justly famous for the steady pursuit of whatever they take in hand, it is notorious that they never lost sight of their design till they had accomplished it, and made themselves entirely masters of these islands, of which they still continue in possession. When this was done, and they had effectually driven out the English, who were likewise settled in them, they fixed the seat of their government in the island of Amboyna, which lay very convenient for the discovery of the southern countries; which, therefore, they prosecuted with great diligence from the year 1619 to the time of Captain Pelsart's shipwreck; that is, for the space of twenty years.

But after they removed the seat of their government from Amboyna to Batavia, they turned their views another way, and never made any voyage expressly for discoveries on that side, except the single one of Captain Tasman, of which we are to speak presently. It was from this period of time that they began to take new measures, and having made their excellent settlement at the Cape of Good Hope, resolved to govern their trade to the East Indies by these two capital maxims: 1. To extend their trade all over the Indies, and to fix themselves so effectually in the richest countries as to keep all, or at least the best and most profitable part of, their commerce to themselves; 2. To make the Moluccas, and the islands dependent on them, their frontier, and to omit nothing that should appear necessary to prevent strangers, or even Dutch ships not belonging to the Company, from ever navigating

B—43

those seas, and consequently from ever being acquainted
with the countries that lie in them. How well they
have prosecuted the first maxim has been very largely
shown in a foregoing article, wherein we have an
ample description of the mighty empire in the hands
of their East India Company. As for the second
maxim, the reader, in the perusal of Funnel's, Dampier's, and other voyages, but especially the first, must
be satisfied that it is what they have constantly at heart,
and which, at all events, they are determined to pursue,
at least with regard to strangers; and as to their own
countrymen, the usage they gave to James le Maire
and his people is a proof that cannot be contested.

Those things being considered, it is very plain that the
Dutch, or rather the Dutch East India Company, are
fully persuaded that they have already as much or more
territory in the East Indies than they can well manage,
and therefore they neither do nor ever will think of
settling New Guinea, Carpentaria, New Holland, or
any of the adjacent islands, till either their trade declines in the East Indies, or they are obliged to exert
themselves on this side to prevent other nations from
reaping the benefits that might accrue to them by their
planting those countries. But this is not all; for as
the Dutch have no thoughts of settling these countries
themselves, they have taken all imaginable pains to
prevent any relations from being published which
might invite or encourage any other nation to make
attempts this way; and I am thoroughly persuaded

that this very account of Captain Pelsart's shipwreck would never have come into the world if it had not been thought it would contribute to this end, or, in other words, would serve to frighten other nations from approaching such an inhospitable coast, everywhere beset with rocks absolutely void of water, and inhabited by a race of savages more barbarous, and, at the same time, more miserable than any other creatures in the world.

The author of this voyage remarks, for the use of seamen, that in the little island occupied by Weybhays, after digging two pits, they were for a considerable time afraid to use the water, having found that these pits ebbed and flowed with the sea; but necessity at last constraining them to drink it, they found it did them no hurt. The reason of the ebbirg and flowing of these pits was their nearness to the sea, the water of which percolated through the sand, lost its saltness, and so became potable, though it followed the motions of the ocean whence it came.

THE VOYAGE OF CAPTAIN ABEL JANSEN TASMAN FOR THE DISCOVERY OF SOUTHERN COUNTRIES.

1642—43.

By direction of the Dutch East India Company. [*Taken from his original Journal.*]

———◦◊◦———

CHAPTER I.

THE OCCASION AND DESIGN OF THIS VOYAGE.

THE great discoveries that were made by the Dutch in these southern countries were subsequent to the famous voyage of Jaques le Maire, who in 1616 passed the straits called by his name ; in 1618. that part of Terra Australis was discovered which the Dutch called Concordia. The next year, the Land of Edels was found, and received its name from its discoverer. In 1620, Batavia was built on the ruins of the old city of Jacatra ; but the seat of government was not immediately removed from Amboyna. In 1622, that part of New Holland which is called Lewin's Land was first found ; and in 1627, Peter Nuyts discovered between New Holland and New Guinea a country which bears his name. There were also some other voyages made, of which, however, we have no sort of account, except that the Dutch were continually beaten in all their attempts to land upon this coast. On their settlement, however, at Batavia, the then general and council of the Indies thought it requisite to have a more perfect survey made of the new-found countries, that the memory of them at least might be preserved, in case no further attempts were made to settle them ; and it was very probably a foresight of few ships going that route any more, which induced such as had then the direction of the Company's affairs to wish that some such survey and description might be made by an able seaman, who was well acquainted with those coasts, and who might be able to add to the discoveries already made, as well as furnish a more accurate description, even of them, than had been hitherto given.

This was faithfully performed by Captain Tasman ; and from the lights afforded by his journal, a very exact and curious map was made of all these new countries. But his voyage was never published entire; and it is very probable that the East India Company never intended it should be published at all. However, Dirk Rembrantz, moved by the excellency and accuracy of the work, published in Low Dutch an extract of Captain Tasman's Journal, which has been ever since considered as a very great curiosity; and, as such, has been translated into many languages, particularly into our own, by the care of the learned Professor of Gresham College, Doctor Hook, an abridgment of which translation found a place in Doctor Harris's Collection of

Voyages. But we have made no use of either of these pieces, the following being a new translation, made with all the care and diligence that is possible.

CHAPTER II.

CAPTAIN TASMAN SAILS FROM BATAVIA, AUGUST 14, 1642.

ON August 14, 1642, I sailed from Batavia with two vessels; the one called the *Heemskirk*, and the other the *Zee-Haan*. On September 5 I anchored at Maurice Island, in the latitude of 20° south, and in the longitude of 83° 48'. I found this island fifty German miles more to the east than I expected; that is to say, 3° 33' of longitude. This island was so called from Prince Maurice, being before known by the name of Cerne. It is about fifteen leagues in circumference, and has a very fine harbour, at the entrance of which there is one hundred fathoms water. The country is mountainous; but the mountains are covered with green trees. The tops of these mountains are so high that they are lost in the clouds, and are frequently covered by thick exhalations or smoke that ascends from them. The air of this island is extremely wholesome. It is well furnished with flesh and fowl; and the sea on its coasts abounds with all sorts of fish. The finest ebony in the world grows here. It is a tall, straight tree of a moderate thickness, covered with a green bark, very thick, under which the wood is as black as pitch, and as close as ivory. There are other trees on the island, which are of a bright red, and a third sort as yellow as wax. The ships belonging to the East India Company commonly touch at this island for refreshments on their passage to Batavia.

I left this island on the 8th of October, and continued my course to the south to the latitude of 40° or 41°, having a strong north-west wind; and finding the needle vary 23, 24, and 25° to the 22nd of October, I sailed from that time to the 29th to the east, inclining a little to the south, till I arrived in the latitude of 45° 47′ south, and in the longitude of 89° 44′; and then observed the variation of the needle to be 26° 45′ towards the west.

As our author was extremely careful in this particular, and observed the variation of the needle with the utmost diligence, it may not be amiss to take this opportunity of explaining this point, so that the importance of his remarks may sufficiently appear. The needle points exactly north only in a few places, and perhaps not constantly in them; but in most it declines a little to the east, or to the west, whence arises eastern and western declination; when this was first observed, it was attributed to certain excavations or hollows in the earth, to veins of lead, stone, and other such-like causes. But when it was found by repeated experiments that this variation varied, it appeared plainly that none of those causes could take place; since if they had, the variation in the same place must always have been the same, whereas the fact is otherwise.

Here at London, for instance, in the year 1580, the variation was observed to be 11° 17' to the east; in the year 1666, the variation was here 34' to the west; and in the year 1734, the variation was somewhat more than 1° west. In order to find the variation of the needle with the least error possible, the seamen take this method: they observe the point the sun is in by the compass, any time after its rising, and then take the altitude of the sun; and in the afternoon they observe when the sun comes to the same altitude, and observe the point the sun is then in by the compass; for the middle, between these two, is the true north or south point of the compass; and the difference between that and the north or south upon the card, which is pointed out by the needle, is the variation of the compass, and shows how much the north and south, given by the compass, deviates from the true north and south points of the horizon. It appears clearly, from what has been said, that in order to arrive at the certain knowledge of the variation, and of the variation of that variation of the compass, it is absolutely requisite to have from time to time distinct accounts of the variation as it is observed in different places: whence the importance of Captain Tasman's remarks, in this respect, sufficiently appears. It is true that the learned and ingenious Dr. Halley has given a very probable account of this matter; but as the probability of that account arises only from its agreement with observations, it follows those are as necessary and as important as ever, in order to strengthen and confirm it.

CHAPTER III.

REMARKS ON THE VARIATION OF THE NEEDLE.

On the 6th of November, I was in 49° 4′ south latitude, and in the longitude of 114° 56′; the variation was at this time 26° westward; and, as the weather was foggy, with hard gales, and a rolling sea from the south-west and from the south, I concluded from thence that it was not at all probable there should be any land between those two points. On November 15th I was in the latitude of 44° 33′ south, and in the longitude of 140° 32′. The variation was then 18° 30′ west, which variation decreased every day, in such a manner, that, on the 21st of the same month, being in the longitude of 158°, I observed the variation to be no more than 4°. On the 22nd of that month, the needle was in continual agitation, without resting in any of the eight points; which led me to conjecture that we were near some mine of loadstone.

This may, at first sight, seem to contradict what has been before laid down, as to the variation, and the

causes of it : but, when strictly considered, they will
be found to agree very well ; for when it is asserted
that veins of loadstone have nothing to do with the
variation of the compass, it is to be understood of the
constant variation of a few degrees to the east, or to
the west : but in cases of this nature, where the variation is absolutely irregular, and the needle plays
quite round the compass, our author's conjecture may
very well find place : yet it must be owned that it is a
point far enough from being clear, that mines of loadstone affect the compass at a distance; which, however,
might be very easily determined, since there are large
mines of loadstone in the island of Elba, on the coast
of Tuscany.

CHAPTER IV.

HE DISCOVERS A NEW COUNTRY TO WHICH HE GIVES THE NAME OF VAN DIEMEN'S LAND.

On the 24th of the same month, being in the latitude of
42° 25′ south, and in the longitude of 163° 50′, I discovered land, which lay east-south-east at the distance
of ten miles, which I called Van Diemen's Land. The
compass pointed right towards this land. The weather
being bad, I steered south and by east along the coast,
to the height of 44° south, where the land runs away
east, and afterwards north-east and by north. In the
latitude of 43° 10′ south, and in the longitude of 167°

55', I anchored on the 1st of December, in a bay, which I called the Bay of Frederic Henry. I heard, or at least fancied I heard, the sound of people upon the shore; but I saw nobody. All I met with worth observing was two trees, which were two fathoms or two fathoms and a half in girth, and sixty or sixty-five feet high from the root to the branches: they had cut with a flint a kind of steps in the bark, in order to climb up to the birds' nests : these steps were the distance of five feet from each other; so that we must conclude that either these people are of a prodigious size, or that they have some way of climbing trees that we are not used to ; in one of the trees the steps were so fresh, that we judged they could not have been cut above four days.

The noise we heard resembled the noise of some sort of trumpet; it seemed to be at no great distance, but we saw no living creature notwithstanding. I perceived also in the sand the marks of 'wild beasts' feet, resembling those of a tiger, or some such creature ; I gathered also some gum from the trees, and likewise some lack. The tide ebbs and flows there about three feet. The trees in this country do not grow very close, nor are they encumbered with bushes or underwood. I observed smoke in several places; however, we did nothing more than set up a post, on which every one cut his name, or his mark, and upon which I hoisted a flag. I observed that in this place the variation was changed to 3° eastward. On December 5th, being

then, by observation, in the latitude of 41° 34', and in
the longitude 169°, I quitted Van Diemen's Land,
and resolved to steer east to the longitude of 195°,
in hopes of discovering the Islands of Solomon.

CHAPTER V.

SAILS FROM THENCE FOR NEW ZEALAND.

ON September 9th I was in the latitude of 42° 37'
south, and in the longitude of 176° 29'; the variation
being there 5° to the east.   On the 12th of the same
month, finding a great rolling sea coming in on the
south-west, I judged there was no land to be hoped
for on that point.   On the 13th, being in the latitude
of 42° 10' south, and in the longitude of 188° 28', I
found the variation 7° 30' eastward.   In this situation
I discovered a high mountainous country, which is at
present marked in the charts under the name of New
Zealand.   I coasted along the shore of this country to
the north-north-east till the 18th; and being then in
the latitude of 40° 50' south, and in the longitude of
191° 41', I anchored in a fine bay, where I observed
the variation to be 9° towards the east.

We found here abundance of the inhabitants: they
had very hoarse voices, and were very large-made
people.   They durst not approach the ship nearer than
a stone's throw; and we often observed them playing

on a kind of trumpet, to which we answered with the instruments that were on board our vessel. These people were of a colour between brown and yellow, their hair long, and almost as thick as that of the Japanese, combed up, and fixed on the top of their heads with a quill, or some such thing, that was thickest in the middle, in the very same manner that Japanese fastened their hair behind their heads. These people cover the middle of their bodies, some with a kind of mat, others with a sort of woollen cloth, but, as for their upper and lower parts, they leave them altogether naked.

On the 19th of December, these savages began to grow a little bolder, and more familiar, insomuch that at last they ventured on board the *Heemskirk* in order to trade with those in the vessel. As soon as I perceived it, being apprehensive that they might attempt to surprise that ship, I sent my shallop, with seven men, to put the people in the *Heemskirk* upon their guard, and to direct them not to place any confidence in those people. My seven men, being without arms, were attacked by these savages, who killed three of the seven, and forced the other four to swim for their lives, which occasioned my giving that place the name of the Bay of Murderers. Our ship's company would, undoubtedly, have taken a severe revenge, if the rough weather had not hindered them. From this bay we bore away east, having the land in a manner all round us. This country appeared to us rich, fertile,

and very well situated, but as the weather was very
foul, and we had at this time a very strong west wind,
we found it very difficult to get clear of the land.

CHAPTER VI.

VISITS THE ISLAND OF THE THREE KINGS, AND
   GOES IN SEARCH OF OTHER ISLANDS DIS-
   COVERED BY SCHOUTEN.

On the 24th of December, as the wind would not
permit us to continue our way to the north, as we
knew not whether we should be able to find a passage
on that side, and as the flood came in from the south-
east, we concluded that it would be the best to return
into the bay, and seek some other way out, but on the
26th, the wind becoming more favourable, we continued our route to the north, turning a little to
the west. On the 4th of January, 1643, being then in
the latitude of 34° 35′ south, and in the longitude of
191° 9′, we sailed quite to the cape, which lies north-
west, where we found the sea rolling in from the
north-east, whence we concluded that we had at last
found a passage, which gave us no small joy. There
was in this strait an island, which we called the
island of the Three Kings; the cape of which we
doubled, with a design to have refreshed ourselves;
but, as we approached it, we perceived on the mountain

thirty or five-and-thirty persons, who, as far as we could discern at such a distance, were men of very large size, and had each of them a large club in his hand: they called out to us in a rough strong voice, but we could not understand anything of what they said. We observed that these people walked at a very great rate, and that they took prodigious large strides. We made the tour of the island, in doing which we saw but very few inhabitants; nor did any of the country seem to be cultivated; we found, indeed, a fresh-water river, and then we resolved to sail east, as far as 220° of longitude; and from thence north, as far as the latitude of 17° south; and thence to the west, till we arrived at the isles of Cocos and Horne, which were discovered by William Schovten, where we intended to refresh ourselves, in case we found no opportunity of doing it before, for though we had actually landed on Van Diemen's Land, we met with nothing there; and, as for New Zealand, we never set foot on it.

In order to render this passage perfectly intelligible it is necessary to observe that the island of Cocos lies in the latitude of 15° 10′ south; and, according to Schovten's account, is well inhabited, and well cultivated, abounding with all sorts of refreshments; but, at the same time, he describes the people as treacherous and base to the last degree. As for the islands of Horne, they lie nearly in the latitude of 15°, are extremely fruitful, and inhabited by people of a kind and gentle disposition, who readily bestowed on the Hollanders whatever refreshments they could ask. It was no wonder, therefore, that, finding themselves thus distressed, Captain Tasman thought of repairing to these islands, where he was sure of obtaining refreshments, either by fair means or otherwise, which design, however, he did not think fit to put in execution.

CHAPTER VII.

REMARKABLE OCCURRENCES IN THE VOYAGE.

ON the 8th of January, being in the latitude of 30° 25′ south, and in the longitude of 192° 20′, we observed the variation of the needle to be 9° towards the east, and as we had a high rolling sea from the south-west, I conjectured there could not be any land hoped for on that side. On the 12th we found ourselves in 30° 5′ south latitude, and in 195° 27′ of longitude, where we found the variation 9° 30′ to the east, a rolling sea from the south-east and from the south-west. It is very plain, from these observations, that the position laid down by Dr. Halley, that the motion of the needle is not governed by the poles of the world, but by other poles, which move round them, is highly probable, for otherwise it is not easy to understand how the needle came to have, as our author affirms it had, a variation of near 27° to the west, in the latitude of 45° 47', and then gradually decreasing till it had no variation at all; after which it turned east, in the latitude of 42° 37', and so continued increasing its variation eastwardly to this time.

CHAPTER VIII.

OBSERVATIONS ON, AND EXPLANATION OF, THE VARIATION OF THE COMPASS.

On the 16th we were in the latitude of 26° 29' south, and in the longitude of 199° 32', the variation of the needle being 8°. Here we are to observe that the eastern variation decreases, which is likewise very agreeable to Doctor Halley's hypothesis; which, in few words, is this: that a certain large solid body contained within, and every way separated from the earth (as having its own proper motion), and being included like a kernel in its shell, revolves circularly from east to west, as the exterior earth revolves the contrary way in the diurnal motion, whence it is easy to explain the position of the four magnetical poles which he attributes to the earth, by allowing two to the nucleus, and two to the exterior earth. And, as the two former perpetually alter the situation by their circular motion, their virtue, compared with the exterior poles, must be different at different times, and consequently the variation of the needle will perpetually change. The doctor attributes to the nucleus an European north pole and an American south one, on account of the variation of variations observed near these places, as being much greater than those found near the two other poles. And he conjectures that these poles will finish their revolution in about seven hundred years, and after that time the same situation of the poles obtain again as at present, and, consequently, the variations will be the same again over all the globe ; so that it requires several ages before this theory can be thoroughly adjusted. He assigns this probable cause of the circular revolution of the nucleus that the diurnal motion, being impressed from without, was not so exactly communicated to the internal parts as to give them the same precise velocity of rotation as the external, whence the nucleus, being left behind by the exterior earth, seems to move slowly in a contrary direction, as from east to west, with regard to the external earth, considered as at rest in respect of the other. But to return to our voyage.

CHAPTER IX.

DISCOVERS A NEW ISLAND, WHICH HE CALLS PYLSTAART ISLAND.

ON the 19th of January, being in the latitude of 22° 35′ south, and in the longitude of 204° 15′, we

had 7° 30′ east variation. In this situation we discovered an island about two or three miles in circumference, which was, as far as we could discern, very
high, steep, and barren. We were very desirous of
coming nearer it, but were hindered by south-east and
south-south-east winds. We called it the Isle of Pyl-
staart, because of the great number of that sort of
birds we saw flying about it, and the next day we saw
two other islands.

CHAPTER X.

AND TWO ISLANDS, TO WHICH HE GIVES THE NAME
OF AMSTERDAM AND ROTTERDAM.

ON the 21st, being in the latitude of 21° 20′ south,
and in the longitude of 205° 29′, we found our variation
7° to the north-east. We drew near to the coast of
the most northern island, which, though not very high,
yet was the larger of the two: we called one of these
islands Amsterdam, and the other Rotterdam. Upon
that of Rotterdam we found great plenty of hogs,
fowls, and all sorts of fruits, and other refreshments.
These islanders did not seem to have the use of arms,
inasmuch as we saw nothing like them in any of their
hands while we were upon the island; the usage they
gave us was fair and friendly, except that they would
steal a little. The current is not very considerable
in this place, where it ebbs north-east, and flows south-

west.   A south-west moon causes a spring-tide, which
rises seven or eight feet at least.   The wind blows
there continually south-east, or south-south-east, which
occasioned the *Heemskirk's* being carried out of the
road, but, however, without any damage.   We did not
fill any water here because it was extremely hard to
get it to the ship.

On the 25th we were in the latitude 20° 15' south,
and in the longitude of 206° 19'.   The variation
here was 6° 20' to the east; and, after having had
sight of several other islands, we made that of Rotterdam : the islanders here resemble those on the island
of Amsterdam.   The people were very good-natured,
parted readily with what they had, did not seem to be
acquainted with the use of arms, but were given to
thieving like the natives of Amsterdam Island.   Here
we took in water, and other refreshments, with all the
conveniency imaginable.   We made the whole circuit
of the island, which we found well-stocked with
cocoa-trees, very regularly planted; we likewise saw
abundance of gardens, extremely well laid out,
plentifully stocked with all kinds of fruit-trees, all
planted in straight lines, and the whole kept in such
excellent order, that nothing could have a better effect
upon the eye.   After quitting the island of Rotterdam,
we had sight of several other islands ; which, however,
did not engage us to alter the resolution we had taken
of sailing north, to the height of 17° south latitude,
and from thence to shape a west course, without going

near either Traitor's Island, or those of Horne, we having then a very brisk wind from the south-east, or east-south-east.

I cannot help remarking upon this part of Captain Tasman's journal, that it is not easy to conceive, unless he was bound up by his instructions, why he did not remain some time either at Rotterdam or at Amsterdam Island, but especially at the former; since, perhaps, there is not a place in the world so happily seated, for making new discoveries with ease and safety. He owns that he traversed the whole island, that he found it a perfect paradise, and that the people gave him not the least cause of being diffident in point of security; so that if his men had thrown up ever so slight a fortification, a part of them might have remained there in safety, while the rest had attempted the discovery of the Islands of Solomon on the one hand, or the continent of De Quiros on the other, from neither of which they were at any great distance, and, from his neglecting this opportunity, I take it for granted that he was circumscribed, both as to his course and to the time he was to employ in these discoveries, by his instructions, for otherwise so able a seaman and so curious a man as his journal shows him to have been, would not certainly have neglected so fair an opportunity.

CHAPTER XI.

AND AN ARCHIPELAGO OF TWENTY SMALL ISLANDS.

On February 6th, being in 17° 19′ of south latitude, and in the longitude of 201° 35′, we found ourselves embarrassed by nineteen or twenty small islands, every one of which was surrounded with sands, shoals, and rocks. These are marked in the charts by the name of Prince William's Islands, or Heemskirk's Shallows. On the 8th we were in the latitude of 15° 29′, and in the longitude of 199° 31′. We had abundance of rain, a strong wind from the north-east, or the north-north-east, with dark cold weather. Fearing, therefore, that we were run farther to the west than we thought ourselves by our reckoning, and dreading that we should fall to the south of New Guinea, or be thrown upon some unknown coast in such blowing misty weather, we resolved to stand away to the north, or to the north-north-west, till we should arrive in the latitude of 4, 5, or 6° south, and then to bear away west for the coast of New Guinea, as the least dangerous way that we could take.

It is very plain from hence, that Captain Tasman had now laid aside all thoughts of discovering farther, and I think it is not difficult to guess at the reason; when he was in this latitude, he was morally certain that he could, without further difficulty, sail round by the coast of New Guinea, and so back again to the East Indies. It is therefore extremely probable that he was directed by his instructions to coast round that great southern continent already discovered, in order to arrive at a certainty whether it was joined to any other part of the world, or whether, notwithstanding its vast extent, viz., from the equator to 43° of south latitude, and from the longitude of 123° to near 190°, it was, notwithstanding, an island. This, I say, was in all appearance the true design of his voyage, and the reason of it seems to be this: that an exact chart being drawn from his discoveries, the East India Company might have perfect intelligence of the extent and situation of this new-found country before they executed the plan they were then contriving for preventing its being visited or farther discovered by their own or any other nation; and this too accounts for the care taken in laying down the map of this country on the pavement of the new stadthouse at Amsterdam; for as this county was henceforward to remain as a kind of deposit or land of reserve in the hands of the East India Company, they took this method of intimating as much to their countrymen, so that, while strangers are gaping at this map as a curiosity, every intelligent Dutchman may say to himself, "Behold the wisdom of the East India Company. By their present empire they support the authority of this republic abroad, and by their extensive commerce enrich its subjects at home, and at the same time show us here what a reserve they have made for the benefit of posterity, whenever, through the vicissitudes to which all sublunary things are liable, their present sources of power and grandeur shall fail."

I cannot help supporting my opinion in this respect, by putting the reader in mind of a very curious piece of ancient history, which furnishes us with the like instance in the conduct of another republic. Diodorus Siculus, in the fifth book of his Historical Library, informs us that in the African Ocean, some days' sail west from Libya, there had been discovered an island, the soil of which was exceedingly fertile and the country no less pleasant, all the land being finely diversified by mountains and plains, the former thick clothed with trees, the latter abounding with fruits and flowers, the whole watered by innumerable rivulets, and affording so pleasant an habitation that a finer or more delightful country fancy itself could not feign; yet he assures us, the Carthagenians, those great masters 'of maritime power and commerce, though they had discovered this admirable island, would never suffer it to be planted, but reserved it as a sanctuary to which they might fly, whenever the ruin of their own republic left them no other resource. This tallies exactly with the policy of the Dutch East India Company, who, if they should at any time be driven from their possessions in Java, Ceylon, and other places in that neighbourhood, would without doubt retire back into the Moluccas, and avail themselves effectually of this noble discovery, which lies open to them, and has been hitherto close shut up to all the world beside. But to proceed.

CHAPTER XII.

OCCURRENCES IN THE VOYAGE.

On February 14th we were in the latitude of 16° 30′ south, and in the longitude of 193° 35′. We had hitherto had much rain and bad weather, but this day the wind sinking, we hailed our consort the *Zee-Haan*, and found to our great satisfaction that our reckonings agreed. On the 20th, in the latitude of 13° 45′, and in the longitude of 193° 35′, we had dark, cloudy weather, much rain, thick fogs, and a rolling sea, on all sides the wind variable. On the 26th, in the latitude of 9° 48′ south, and in the longitude of 193° 43′, we had a north-west wind, having every day, for the space of twenty-one days, rained more or less. On March 2nd, in the latitude of 9° 11′ south, and in the longitude of 192° 46′, the variation was 10° to the east, the wind and weather still varying. On March 8th, in the latitude of 7° 46′ south, and in the longitude of 190° 47′, the wind was still variable.

CHAPTER XIII.

HE ARRIVES AT THE ARCHIPELAGO OF ANTHONG
JAVA.

ON the 14th, in the latitude of 10° 12′ south, and in
the longitude of 186° 14′, we found the variation 8°
45′ to the east. We passed some days without being
able to take any observation, because the weather was
all that time dark and rainy. On March 20th, in the
latitude of 5° 15′ south, and in the longitude of 181°
16′, the weather being then fair, we found the variation
9° eastward. On the 22nd, in the latitude of 5° 2′
south, and in the longitude of 178° 32′, we had fine
fair weather, and the benefit of the east trade wind.
This day we had sight of land, which lay four miles
west. This land proved to be a cluster of twenty
islands, which in the maps are called Anthong Java.
They lie ninety miles or thereabouts from the coast of
New Guinea. It may not be amiss to observe here,
that what Captain Tasman calls the coast of New
Guinea, is in reality the coast of New Britain, which
Captain Dampier first discovered to be a large island
separated from the coast of New Guinea.

CHAPTER XIV.

HIS ARRIVAL ON THE COAST OF NEW GUINEA.

ON the 25th, in the latitude of 4° 35′ south, and in the longitude of 175° 10′, we found the variation 9° 30′ east. We were then in the height of the islands of Mark, which were discovered by William Schovten and James le Maire. They are fourteen or fifteen in number, inhabited by savages, with black hair, dressed and trimmed in the same manner as those we saw before at the Bay of Murderers in New Zealand. On the 29th we passed the Green Islands, and on the 30th that of St. John, which were likewise discovered by Schovten and Le Maire. This island they found to be of a considerable extent, and judged it to lie at the distance of one thousand eight hundred and forty leagues from the coast of Peru. It appeared to them well inhabited and well cultivated, abounding with flesh, fowl, fish, fruit, and other refreshments. The inhabitants made use of canoes of all sizes, were armed with slings, darts, and wooden swords, wore necklaces and bracelets of pearl, and rings in their noses. They were, however, very intractable, notwithstanding all the pains that could be taken to engage them in a fair correspondence, so that Captain Schovten was at last obliged to fire upon them to prevent them from making themselves masters of his vessel, which they attacked with a great deal of vigour; and very probably this was the reason that Captain Tasman did not attempt to land or make any farther discovery. On April 1st, we were in the latitude of 4° 30′ south, and in the longitude of 171° 2′, the variation being 8° 45′ to the east, having now sight of the coast of New Guinea; and endeavouring to double the cape which the Spaniards call Cobo Santa Maria, we continued to sail along the coast which lies north-west. We afterwards passed the islands of Antony Caens, Gardeners Island, and Fishers Island, advancing towards the promontory called Struis Hoek, where the coast runs south and south-east. We resolved to pursue the same route, and to continue steering south till we should either discover land or a passage on that side.

It is necessary to observe, that all this time they continued on the coast, not of New Guinea but of New Britain, for that cape which the Spaniards called Santa Maria is the very same that Captain Dampier called Cape St. George, and Caens, Gardeners, and Fishers Islands all lie upon the same coast. They had been discovered by Schovten and Le Maire, who found them to be well inhabited, but by a very base and treacherous people, who, after making signs of peace, attempted to surprise their ships; and these islanders managed their slings with such force and dexterity, as to drive the Dutch sailors from their decks; which account of Le Maire's agree perfectly well with what Captain Dampier tells us of the same people. As for the continent of New Guinea, it lies quite behind the island of New Britain, and was therefore laid down in all the charts before Dampier's discovery, at least four degrees more to the east than it should have been.

CHAPTER XV.

CONTINUES HIS VOYAGE ALONG THAT COAST.

ON April 12th, in the latitude of 3° 45′ south, and in the longitude of 167°, we found the variation 10° towards the east. That night part of the crew were wakened out of their sleep by an earthquake. They immediately ran upon deck, supposing that the ship had struck. On heaving the lead, however, there was no bottom to be found. We had afterwards several shocks, but none of them so violent as the first. We had then doubled the Struis Hoek, and were at that time in the Bay of Good Hope. On the 14th, in the latitude of 5° 27′ south, and in the longitude of 166° 57′, we observed the variation to be 9° 15′ to the east. The land lay then north-east, east-north-east, and again south-south-west, so that we imagined there had been a passage between those two points; but we were soon convinced of our mistake, and that it was all one coast, so that we were obliged to double the West Cape and to continue creeping along shore, and were much hindered in our passage by calms. This description agrees very well with that of Schovten and Le Maire, so that probably they had now sight again of the coast of New Guinea.

It is very probable, from the accident that happened to Captain Tasman, and which also happened to others upon that coast, and from the burning mountains that will be hereafter mentioned, that this country is very subject to earthquakes, and if so, without doubt it abounds with metals and minerals, of which we have also another proof from a point in which all these writers agree, viz., that the people they saw had rings in their noses and ears, though none of them tell us of what metal those rings were made, which Le Maire might easily have done, since he carried off a man from one of the islands whose name was Moses, from whom he learned that almost every nation on this coast speaks a different language.

CHAPTER XVI.

ARRIVES IN THE NEIGHBOURHOOD OF BURNING ISLAND, AND SURVEYS THE WHOLE COAST OF NEW GUINEA.

ON the 20th, in the latitude of 5° 4′ south, and in the longitude 164° 27′, we found the variation 8° 30′ east. We that night drew near the Brandande Yland, i.e., burning island, which William Schovten mentions, and we perceived a great flame issuing, as he says, from the top of a high mountain.   When we were between that island and the continent, we saw a vast number of fires along the shore and half-way up the mountain, from whence we concluded that the country must be very populous. We were often detained on this coast by calms, and frequently observed small trees, bamboos, and shrubs, which the rivers on that coast carried into the sea; from which we inferred that this part of the country was extremely well watered, and that the land must be very good. The next morning we passed the burning mountain, and continued a west-north-west course along that coast.

It is remarkable that Schovten had made the same observation with respect to the drift-wood forced by the rivers into the sea. He likewise observed that there was so copious a discharge of fresh water, that it altered the colour and the taste of the sea. He likewise says that the burning island is extremely well peopled, and also well cultivated. He afterwards anchored on the coast of the continent, and endeavoured to trade with the natives, who made him pay very dear for hogs and cocoa-nuts, and likewise showed him some ginger. It appears from Captain Tasman's account that he was now in haste to return to Batavia, and did not give himself so much trouble as at the beginning about discoveries, and to say the truth, there was no great occasion, if, as I observed, his commission was no more than to sail round the new discovered coasts, in order to lay them down with greater certainty in the Dutch charts.

CHAPTER XVII.

COMES TO THE ISLANDS OF JAMA AND MOA.

ON the 27th, being in the latitude of 2° 10′ south, and in the longitude of 146° 57′, we fancied that we had a sight of the island of Moa, but it proved to be that of Jama, which lies a little to the east of Moa. We found here great plenty of cocoa-nuts and other refreshments. The inhabitants were absolutely black, and could easily repeat the words that they heard others speak, which shows their own to be a very copious language. It is, however, exceedingly difficult to pronounce, because they make frequent use of the letter R, and sometimes to such a degree that it occurs twice or thrice in the same word. The next day we anchored on the coast of the island of Moa, where we likewise found abundance of refreshments, and where we were obliged by bad weather to stay till May 9th. We purchased there, by way of exchange, six thousand cocoa-nuts, and a hundred bags of pysanghs or Indian figs. When we first began to trade with these people, one of our seamen was wounded by an arrow that one of the natives let fly, either through malice or inadvertency. We were at that very juncture endeavouring to bring our ships close to the shore, which so terrified these islanders, that they brought of their own accord on board us, the man who had shot the arrow and left him at our mercy. We found them

.fter this accident much more tractable than before in
every respect. Our sailors, therefore, pulled off the
iron hoops from some of the old water-casks, stuck
them into wooden handles, and filing them to an edge,
sold these awkward knives to the inhabitants for their
fruits.

In all probability they had not forgot what happened
to our people on July 16th, 1616, in the days of William
Schovten : these people, it seems, treated him very ill;
upon which James le Maire brought his ship close to
the shore, and fired a broadside through the woods;
the bullets, flying through the trees, struck the negroes
with such a panic, that they fled in an instant up
into the country, and durst not show their heads again
till they had made full satisfaction for what was past,
and thereby secured their safety for the time to come;
and he traded with them afterwards very peaceably,
and with mutual satisfaction.

This account of our author's seems to have been
taken upon memory, and is not very exact. Schovten's
seamen, or rather the petty officer who commanded his
long boat, insulted the natives grossly before they
offered any injury to his people; and then, notwithstanding they fired upon them with small arms, the
islanders obliged them to retreat; so that they were
forced to bring the great guns to bear upon the island
before they could reduce them. These people do not
deserve to be treated as savages, because Schovten
acknowledges that they had been engaged in commerce

c—43

with the Spaniards ; as appeared by their having iron
pots, glass beads, and pendants, with other European
commodities, before he came thither.   He also tells us
that they were a very civilised people, their country well
cultivated and very fruitful; that they had a great many
boats, and other small craft, which they navigated with
great dexterity.   He adds also, that they gave him a
very distinct account of the neighbouring islands, and
that they solicited him to fire upon the Arimoans, with
whom it seems they are always at war; which, however,
he refused to do, unless provoked to it by some injury
offered by those people.   It is therefore very apparent
that the inhabitants of Moa are a people with whom
any Europeans, settled in their neighbourhood, might
without any difficulty settle a commerce, and receive
considerable assistance from them in making discoveries.   But perhaps some nations are fitter for these
kind of expeditions than others, as being less apt to
make use of their artillery and small arms upon every
little dispute; for as the inhabitants of Moa are well
enough acquainted with the superiority which the
Europeans have over them, it cannot be supposed that
they will ever hazard their total destruction by com-
mitting any gross act of cruelty upon strangers who
visit their coast; and it is certainly very unfair to
treat people as savages and barbarians, merely for
defending themselves when insulted or attacked without cause.   The instance Captain Tasman gives us of
their delivering up the man who wounded his sailor is

a plain proof of this ; and as to the diffidence and suspicion which some later voyagers have complained of
with respect to the inhabitants of this island, they
must certainly be the effects of the bad behaviour of
such Europeans as this nation have hitherto dealt with,
and would be effectually removed, if ever they had a
settled experience of a contrary conduct.   The surest
method of teaching people to behave honestly towards
us is to behave friendly and honestly towards them, and
then there is no great reason to fear, that such as give
evident proofs of capacity and civility in the common
affairs of life should be guilty of treachery that must
turn to their own disadvantage.

CHAPTER XVIII.

PROSECUTES HIS VOYAGE TO CERAM.

ON the 12th of May, being then in the latitude of 54′
south, and in the longitude of 153° 17′, we found the
variation 6° 30′ to the east.   We continued coasting
the north side of the island of William Schovten,
which is about eighteen or nineteen miles long, very
populous, and the people very brisk and active.   It
was with great caution that Schovten gave his name to
this island, for having observed that there were abundance of small islands laid down in the charts on the
coast of New Guinea, he was suspicious that this might

be of the number. But since that time it seems a point generally agreed, that this island had not before any particular name; and therefore, in all subsequent voyages, we find it constantly mentioned by the name of Schovten's Island.

He describes it as a very fertile and well-peopled island; the inhabitants of which were so far from discovering anything of a savage nature, that they gave apparent testimonies of their having had an extensive commerce before he touched there, since they not only showed him various commodities from the Spaniards, but also several samples of China ware; he observes that they are very unlike the nations he had seen before, being rather of an olive colour than black; some having short, others long hair, dressed after different fashions; they were also a taller, stronger, and stouter people than their neighbours. These little circumstances. which may seem tedious or trifling to such as read only for amusement, are, however, of very great importance to such as have discoveries in view; because they argue that these people have a general correspondence; the difference of their complexion must arise from a mixed descent; and the different manner of wearing their hair is undoubtedly owing to their following the fashion of different nations, as their fancies lead them. He farther observes that their vessels were larger and better contrived than their neighbours; that they readily parted with their bows and arrows in exchange for goods, and that they were particularly fond of glass and ironware, which, perhaps, they not only used themselves, but employed likewise in their commerce. The most western point of the island he called the Cape of Good Hope, because by doubling that cape he expected to reach the island of Banda; and that we may not wonder that he was in doubts and difficulties as to the situation of these places, we ought to reflect that Schovten was the first who sailed round the world by this course, and the last too, except Commodore Roggewein, other navigators choosing rather to run as high as California, and from thence to the Ladrone Islands, merely because it is the ordinary route.

In the neighbourhood of this island Schovten also met with an earthquake, which alarmed the ship's company excessively, from an apprehension that they had struck upon a rock. There are some other islands in the neighbourhood of this, well peopled, and well planted, abounding with excellent fruits, especially of the melon kind. These islands lie, as it were, on the confines of the southern continent, and the East Indies, so that the inhabitants enjoy all the advantages resulting from their own happy climate, and from their traffic with their neighbours, especially with those of Ternate and Amboyna, who come thither yearly to purchase their commodities, and who are likewise visited at certain seasons by the people of these islands in their turn.

CHAPTER XIX.

ON the 18th of May, in the latitude of 26' south and in
the longitude of 147° 55', we observed the variation to
be 5° 30' east. We were now arrived at the western
extremity of New Guinea, which is a detached point
or promontory (though it is not marked so even in the
latest maps); here we met with calms, variable and
contrary winds, with much rain; from thence we steered
for Ceram, leaving the Cape on the north, and arrived
safely on that island; by this time Captain Tasman
had fairly surrounded the continent he was instructed
to discover, and had therefore nothing now farther in
view than to return to Batavia, in order to report the
discoveries he had made.

On the 27th of May we passed through the straits
of Boura, or Bouton, and continued our passage to
Batavia, where we arrived on the 15th of June, in
the latitude of 6° 12' south, and in the longitude of
127° 18'. This voyage was made in the space of ten
months. Such was the end of this expedition, which
has been always considered as the clearest and most
exact that was ever made for the discovery of the Terra
Australis Incognita, from whence that chart and map
was laid down in the pavement of the stadt-house at
Amsterdam, as is before mentioned. We have now
nothing to do but to shut up this voyage and our

history of circumnavigators, with a few remarks, previous to which it will be requisite to state clearly and succinctly the discoveries, either made or confirmed by Captain Tasman's voyage, that the importance of it may fully appear, as well as the probability of our conjectures with regard to the motives that induced the Dutch East India Company to be at so much pains about these discoveries.

CHAPTER XX.

CONSEQUENCES OF CAPTAIN TASMAN'S DISCOVERIES.

IN the first place, then, it is most evident, from Captain Tasman's voyage, that New Guinea, Carpentaria, New Holland, Antony van Diemen's Land, and the countries discovered by De Quiros, make all one continent, from which New Zealand seems to be separated by a strait; and, perhaps, is part of another continent, answering to Africa, as this, of which we are now speaking, plainly does to America. This continent reaches from the equinoctial to 44° of south latitude, and extends from 122° to 188° of longitude, making indeed a very large country, but nothing like what De Quiros imagined; which shows how dangerous a thing it is to trust too much to conjecture in such points as these. It is, secondly, observable, that as New Guinea, Carpentaria, and New Holland, had been already pretty well examined, Captain Tasman fell directly to the south of these; so that his first discovery was Van Diemen's Land, the most southern part of the continent on this side the globe, and then passing round by New Zealand, he plainly discovered the opposite side of that country towards America, though he visited the islands only, and never fell in again with the continent till he arrived on the coast of New Britain, which he mistook for that of New Guinea, as he very well might; that country having never been suspected to be an island, till Dampier discovered it to be such in the beginning of the present century. Thirdly, by this survey, these countries are for ever marked out, so long as the map, or memory of this voyage, shall remain. The Dutch East India Company have it always in their power to direct settlements, or new discoveries, either in New Guinea, from the Moluccas, or in New Holland, from Batavia directly. The prudence shown in the conduct of this affair deserves the highest praise. To have attempted heretofore, or even now, the establishing colonies in those countries, would be impolitic, because it would be grasping more than the East India Company, or than even the republic of Holland, could manage; for, in the first place, to reduce a continent between three and four thousand miles broad is a prodigious undertaking, and to settle it by degrees would be to open to all the world the importance of that country which, for anything we can tell, may be much superior to any country yet known : the only choice,

therefore, that the Dutch had left, was to reserve this
mighty discovery till the season arrived, in which they
should be either obliged by necessity or invited by
occasion to make use of it; but though this country
be reserved. it is no longer either unknown or neglected by the Dutch, which is a point of very great
consequence.   To the other nations of Europe, the
southern continent is a chimera, a thing in the clouds,
or at least a country about which there are a thousand
doubts and suspicions, so that to talk of discovering or
settling it must be regarded as an idle and empty project:
but, with respect to them, it is a thing perfectly well
known; its extent, its boundaries, its situation, the
genius of its several nations, and the commodities of
which they are possessed, are absolutely within their
cognisance, so that they are at liberty to take such
measures as appear to them best, for securing the
eventual possession of this country, whenever they
think fit.   This account explains at once all the
mysteries which the best writers upon this subject
have found in the Dutch proceedings.   It shows why
they have been at so much pains to obtain a clear and
distinct survey of these distant countries; why they
have hitherto forborne settling, and why they take so
much pains to prevent other nations from coming at a
distinct knowledge of them: and I may add to this
another particular, which is that it accounts for their
permitting the natives of Amboyna, who are their subjects, to carry on a trade to New Guinea, and the adjacent

countries, since, by this very method, it is apparent that they gain daily fresh intelligence as to the product and commodities of those countries. Having thus explained the consequence of Captain Tasman's voyage, and thereby fully justified my giving it a place in this part of my work, I am now at liberty to pursue the reflections with which I promised to close this section, and the history of circumnavigators, and in doing which, I shall endeavour to make the reader sensible of the advantages that arise from publishing these voyages in their proper order, so as to show what is, and what is yet to be discovered of the globe on which we live.

CHAPTER XXI.

REMARKS UPON THE VOYAGE.

IN speaking of the consequences of Captain Tasman's voyage, it has been very amply shown that this part of Terra Australis, or southern country, has been fully and certainly discovered. To prevent, however, the reader's making any mistake, I will take this opportunity of laying before him some remarks on the whole southern hemisphere, which will enable him immediately to comprehend all that I have afterwards to say on this subject.

If we suppose the south pole to be the centre of a

chart of which the equinoctial is the circumference, we shall then discern four quarters, of the contents of which, if we could give a full account, this part of the world would be perfectly discovered. To begin then with the first of these, that is, from the first meridian, placed in the island of Fero. Within this division, that is to say, from the first to the nineteenth degree of longitude, there lies the great continent of Africa, the most southern point of which is the Cape of Good Hope, lying in the latitude of 34° 15′ south. Between that and the pole, several small but very inconsiderable islands have been discovered, affording us only this degree of certainty, that to the latitude of 50° there is no land to be found of any consequence; there was, indeed, a voyage made by Mr. Bovet in the year 1738, on purpose to discover whether there were any lands to the south in that quarter or not. This gentleman sailed from Port l'Orient July the 18th, 1738, and on the 1st of January, 1739, discovered a country, the coasts of which were covered with ice, in the latitude of 54° south, and in the longitude of 28° 30′, the variation of the compass being there 6° 45′, to the west.

In the next quarter, that is to say, from 90° longitude to 180°, lie the countries of which we have been speaking, or that large southern island, extending from the equinoctial to the latitude of 43° 10′, and the longitude of 167° 55′, which is the extremity of Van Diemen's Land.

In the third quarter, that is, from the longitude of

150° to 170°, there is very little discovered with any certainty. Captain Tasman, indeed, visited the coast of New Zealand, in the latitude of 42° 10′ south, and in the longitude of 188° 28′ ; but besides this, and the islands of Amsterdam and Rotterdam, we know very little; and therefore, if there be any doubts about the reality of Terra Australis, it must be with respect to that part of it which lies within this quarter, through which Schovten and Le Maire sailed, but without discovering anything more than a few small islands.

The fourth and last quarter is from 270° of longitude to the first meridian, within which lies the continent of South America, and the island of Terra del Fuego, the most southern promontory of which is supposed to be Cape Horn, which, according to the best of observations, is in the latitude of 56°, beyond which there has been nothing with any degree of certainty discovered on this side.

On the whole, therefore, it appears there are three continents already tolerably discovered which point towards the south pole, and therefore it is very probable there is a fourth, which if there be, it must lie between the country of New Zealand, discovered by Captain Tasman, and that country which was seen by Captain Sharpe and Mr. Wafer in the South Seas, to which land therefore, and no other, the title of Terra Australis Incognita properly belongs. Leaving this, therefore, to the industry of future ages to discover, we will now return to that great southern island which

Captain Tasman actually surrounded, and the bounds of which are tolerably well known.

In order to give the reader a proper idea of the importance of this country, it will be requisite to say something of the climates in which it is situated. As it lies from the equinoctial to near the latitude of 44°, the longest day in the most northern parts must be twelve hours, and in the southern about fifteen hours, or somewhat more, so that it extends from the first to the seventh climate, which shows its situation to be the happiest in the world, the country called Van Diemen's Land resembling in all respects the south of France. As there are in all countries some parts more pleasant than others, so there seems good reason to believe that within two or three degrees of the tropic of Capricorn, which passes through the midst of New Holland, is the most unwholesome and disagreeable part of this country; the reason of which is very plain, for in those parts it must be excessively hot, much more so than under the line itself, since the days and nights are there always equal, whereas within three or four degrees of the tropic of Capricorn, that is to say, in the latitude 27° south, the days are thirteen hours and a half long, and the sun is twice in their zenith, first in the beginning of December, or rather in the latter end of November, and again when it returns back, which occasions a burning heat for about two months, or something more; whereas, either farther to the south or nearer to the line, the climate must be equally wholesome and pleasant.

As to the product and commodities of this country in general, there is the greatest reason in the world to believe that they are extremely rich and valuable, because the richest and finest countries in the known world lie all of them within the same latitude; but 'to return from conjectures to facts, the country discovered by De Quiros makes a part of this great island, and is the opposite coast to that of Carpentaria. This country, the discoverer called La Australia del Espiritu Santo, in the latitude of 15° 40' south, and, as he reports, it abounds with gold, silver, pearl, nutmegs, mace, ginger, and sugar-canes, of an extraordinary size. I do not wonder that formerly the fact might be doubted, but at present I think there is sufficient reason to induce us to believe it, for Captain Dampier describes the country about Cape St. George and Port Mountague, which are within 9° of the country described by De Quiros. I say Captain Dampier describes what he saw in the following words: "The country hereabouts is mountainous and woody, full of rich valleys and pleasant fresh-water brooks; the mould in the valleys is deep and yellowish, that on the sides of the hills of a very brown colour, and not very deep, but rocky underneath, yet excellent planting land; the trees in general are neither very straight, thick, nor tall, yet appear green and pleasant enough; some of them bear flowers, some berries, and others big fruits, but all unknown to any of us; cocoa-nut trees thrive very well here, as well on the bays by the sea-side, as more remote among

the plantations; the nuts are of an indifferent size, the
milk and kernel very thick and pleasant; here are
ginger, yams, and other very good roots for the pot,
that our men saw and tasted; what other fruits or
roots the country affords I know not; here are hogs
and dogs, other land animals we saw none; the fowls
we saw and knew were pigeons, parrots, cocadores, and
crows, like those in England; a sort of birds about the
bigness of a blackbird, and smaller birds many. The
sea and rivers have plenty of fish; we saw abundance,
though we catched but few, and these were cavallies,
yellow-tails, and whip-wreys."

This account is grounded only on a very slight view,
whereas De Quiros resided for some time in the place
he has mentioned. In another place Captain Dampier
observes that he saw nutmegs amongst them, which
seemed to be fresh-gathered, all which agrees perfectly
with the account given by De Quiros; add to this,
that Schovten had likewise observed, that they had
ginger upon this coast, and some other spices, so that
on the whole there seems not the least reason to doubt
that if any part of this country was settled, it must be
attended with a very rich commerce; for it cannot be
supposed that all these writers should be either mis-
taken, or that they should concur in a design to impose
upon their readers; which is the less to be suspected,
if we consider how well their reports agree with the
situation of the country, and that the trees on the
land, and the fish on the coast, corresponding exactly

with the trees of those countries, and the fish on the coasts, where these commodities are known to abound within land, seem to intimate a perfect conformity throughout.

The next thing to be considered is, the possibility of planting in this part of the world, which at first sight, I must confess, seems to be attended with considerable difficulties with respect to every other nation except the Dutch, who either from Batavia, the Moluccas, or even from the Cape of Good Hope, might with ease settle themselves wherever they thought fit; as, however, they have neglected this for above a century, there seems to be no reason why their conduct in this respect should become the rule of other nations, or why any other nation should be apprehensive of drawing on herself the displeasure of the Dutch, by endeavouring to turn to their benefit countries the Dutch have so long suffered to lie, with respect to Europe, waste and desert.

The first point, with respect to a discovery, would be to send a small squadron on the coast of Van Diemen's Land, and from thence round, in the same course taken by Captain Tasman, by the coast of New Guinea, which might enable the nations that attempted it to come to an absolute certainty with regard to its commodities and commerce. Such a voyage as this might be performed with very great ease, and at a small expense, by our East India Company; and this in the space of eight or nine months' time; and considering what mighty advantages might accrue to the nation, there seems to be nothing harsh or improbable in supposing that some time or other, when the legislature is more than usually intent on affairs of commerce, they may be directed to make such an expedition at the expense of the public. By this means all the back coast of New Holland and New Guinea might be thoroughly examined, and we might know as well, and as certainly as the Dutch, how far a colony settled there might answer our expectations; one thing is certain, that to persons used to the navigation of the Indies, such an expedition could not be thought either dangerous or difficult, because it is already sufficiently known that there are everywhere islands upon the coast, where ships upon such a discovery might be sure to meet with refreshments, as is plain from Commodore Roggewein's voyage, made little more than twenty years ago.

The only difficulty that I can see would be the getting a fair and honest account of this expedition when made; for private interest is so apt to interfere, and get the better of the public service, that it is very hard to be sure of anything of this sort. That I may not be suspected of any intent to calumniate, I shall put the reader in mind of two instances; the first is, as to the new trade from Russia, for establishing of which an Act of Parliament was with great difficulty obtained, though visibly for the advantage of the nation; the other instance is, the voyage of Captain

Middleton, for the discovery of a north-west passage
into the south seas, which is ended by a very warm
dispute, whether that passage be found or not, the
person supposed to have found it maintaining the
negative.

Whenever, therefore, such an expedition is under-
taken, it ought to be under the direction, not only of
a person of parts and experience, but of unspotted
character, who, on his return, should be obliged to
deliver his journal upon oath, and the principal officers
under him should likewise be directed to keep their
journals distinctly, and without their being inspected
by the principal officer; all which journals ought to be
published by authority as soon as received, that every
man might be at liberty to examine them, and deliver
his thoughts as to the discoveries made, or the impedi-
ments suggested to have hindered or prevented such
discoveries, by which means the public would be sure
to obtain a full and distinct account of the matter; and
it would thence immediately appear whether it would
be expedient to prosecute the design or not.

But if it should be thought too burdensome for a
company in so flourishing a condition, and consequently
engaged in so extensive a commerce as the East India
Company is, to undertake such an expedition, merely
to serve the public, promote the exportation of our
manufactures, and increase the number of industrious
persons who are maintained by foreign trade; if this,
I say, should be thought too grievous for a company

that has purchased her privileges from the public by a
large loan at low interest, there can certainly be no
objection to the putting this project into the hands of
the Royal African Company, who are not quite in so
flourishing a condition; they have equal opportunities
for undertaking it, since the voyage might be with
great ease performed from their settlements in ten
months, and if the trade was found to answer, it might
encourage the settling a colony at Madagascar to and
from which ships might, with the greatest conveniency,
carry on the trade to New Guinea. I cannot say how
far such a trade might be consistent with their present
charter; but if it should be found advantageous to the
public, and beneficial to the company, I think there can
be no reason assigned why it should not be secured to
them, and that too in the most effectual manner.

A very small progress in it would restore the reputation of the company, and in time, perhaps, free the
nation from the annual expense she is now at, for the
support of the forts and garrisons belonging to that
company on the coasts of Africa; which would alone
prove of great and immediate service, both to the public
and to the company. To say the truth, something of
this sort is absolutely necessary to vindicate the expense
the nation is at; for if the trade, for the carrying on
of which a company is established, proves, by a change
of circumstances, incapable of supporting that company,
and thereby brings a load upon the public, this ought
to be a motive, it ought, indeed, to be the strongest

motive, for that company to endeavour the extension of
its commerce, or the striking out, if possible, some new
branch of trade, which may restore it to its former
splendour; and in this as it hath an apparent right, so
there is not the least reason to doubt that it would
meet with all the countenance and assistance from the
government that it could reasonably expect or desire.

If such a design should ever be attempted, perhaps
the island of New Britain might be the properest place
for them to settle. As to the situation, extent, and
present condition of that island, all that can be said
of it must be taken from the account given by its
discoverer Captain Dampier, which, in few words,
amounts to this: "The island which I call Nova
Britannia has about 4° of latitude, the body of it lying
in 4°, the northernmost part in 2° 30', and the southernmost in 6° 30'. It has about 5° 18' longitude from
east to west; it is generally high mountainous land,
mixed with large valleys, which, as well as the
mountains, appeared very fertile; and in most places
that we saw the trees are very large, tall, and thick.
It is also very well inhabited with strong, well-limbed
negroes, whom we found very daring and bold at several
places: as to the product of it, it is very probable this
island may afford as many rich commodities as any in
the world; and the natives may be easily brought to
commerce, though I could not pretend to it in my
circumstances." If any objections should be raised
from Dampier's misfortune in that voyage, it is easy

to show that it ought to have no manner of weight whatever, since, though he was an excellent pilot, he is allowed to have been but a bad commander; besides, the *Roebuck*, in which he sailed, was a worn-out frigate that would hardly swim; and it is no great wonder that in so crazy a vessel the people were a little impatient at being abroad on discoveries; yet, after all, he performed what he was sent for; and, by the discovery of this island of New Britain, secured us an indisputable right to a country, that is, or might be made, very valuable.

It is so situated, that a great trade might be carried on from thence through the whole Terra Australis on one side, and the most valuable islands of the East Indies on the other. In short, all, or at least most, of the advantages proposed by the Dutch West India Company's joining with their East India Company, of which a large account has already been given, might be procured for this nation, by the establishing a colony in this island of New Britain, and securing the trade of that colony to the African Company by law; the very passing of which law would give the company more than sufficient credit, to fit out a squadron at once capable of securing the possession of that island, and of giving the public such satisfaction as to its importance, as might be requisite to obtain further power and assistance from the State, if that should be found necessary. It would be very easy to point out some advantages peculiarly convenient for that company; but it

will be time enough to think of these whenever the
African Company shall discover an inclination to
prosecute this design. At present I have done what I
proposed, and have shown that such a collection of
voyages as this ought not to be considered as a work
of mere amusement, but as a work calculated for the
benefit of mankind in general, and of this nation in
particular, which it is the duty of every man to promote in his station ; and whatever fate these reflections
may meet with, I shall always have the satisfaction of
remembering that I have not neglected it in mine, but
have taken the utmost pains to turn a course of labo-
rious reading to the advantage of my country.

But, supposing that neither of these companies
should think it expedient, or, in other words, should
not think it consistent with their interest to attempt
this discovery, there is yet a third company, within the
spirit of whose charter, I humbly conceive, the prosecution of such a scheme immediately lies. The reader
will easily discern that I mean the company for carrying on a trade to the South Seas, who, notwithstanding
the extensiveness of their charter, confirmed and supported by authority of parliament, have not, so far as
my information reaches, ever attempted to send so
much as a single ship for the sake of discoveries into
the South Seas, which, however, was the great point
proposed when this company was first established. In
order to prove this, I need only lay before the reader
the limits assigned that company by their charter, the

substance of which is contained in the following words :—

" The corporation, and their successors, shall, for ever, be vested in the sole trade into and from all the kingdoms and lands on the east side of America, from the River Oroonoco, to the southernmost part of Terra del Fuego, and on the west side thereof from the said southernmost part of Terra del Fuego, through the South Sea, to the northernmost part of America, and into and through all the countries, islands, and places within the said limits, which are reputed to belong to Spain, or which shall hereafter be found out and discovered within the limits aforesaid, not exceeding 300 leagues from the continent of America, between the southernmost part of the Terra del Fuego and the northernmost part of America, on the said west side thereof, except the Kingdom of Brazil, and such other places on the east side of America, as are now in the possession of the King of Portugal, and the country of Surinam, in the possession of the States-general. The said company, and none else, are to trade within the said limits; and, if any other persons shall trade to the South Seas, they shall forfeit the ship and goods, and double value, one-fourth part to the crown, and another fourth part to the prosecutor, and the other two-fourths to the use of the company. And the company shall be the sole owners of the islands, forts, etc., which they shall discover within the said limits, to be held of the crown, under an annual rent of an ounce of gold, and of all ships taken as prizes by the ships of the said company; and the company may seize, by force of arms, all other British ships trading in those seas."

It is, I think, impossible for any man to imagine that either these limits should be secured to the company for no purpose in the world; or that these prohibitions and penalties should take place, notwithstanding the company's never attempting to make any use of these powers; from whence I infer that it was the intent of the legislature that new discoveries should be made, new plantations settled, and a new trade carried on by this new corporation, agreeable to the rules prescribed, and for the general benefit of this nation; which I apprehend was chiefly considered in the providing that this new commerce should be put under the management of a particular company. But I am very well aware of an objection that may be made to what I have advanced; viz., that, from my own showing, this southern continent lies absolutely without their limits; and that there is also a proviso in the charter of that company that seems particularly calculated to exclude it, since it recites that

" The agents of the company shall not sail beyond the southernmost parts of Terra del Fuego, except through the Straits of Magellan, or round Terra del Fuego; nor go from thence to any part of the East Indies, nor return to Great Britain, or any port or place, unless through the said straits, or by Terra del Fuego: nor shall they trade in East India goods, or in any

places within the limits granted to the united company
of merchants of England trading to East India (such
India goods excepted as shall be actually exported from
Great Britain, and also such gold, silver, wrought
plate, and other goods and commodities, which are the
produce, growth, or manufactures of the West Indies,
or continent of America): neither shall they send
ships, or use them or any vessel, within the South Seas,
from Terra del Fuego to the northernmost parts of
America, above three hundred leagues to the westward
of, and distant from the land of Chili, Peru, Mexico,
California, or any other the lands or shores of Southern
or Northern America, between Terra del Fuego and
the northernmost part of America, on pain of the for-
feiture of the ships and goods; one-third to the crown,
and the other two-thirds to the East India Company."

But the reader will observe that I mentioned the
East India and African Companies before; and that I
now mention the South Sea Company, on a supposition
that the two former may refuse it. In that case, I
presume, the legislature will make the same distinction
that the States of Holland did, and not suffer the
private advantage of any particular company to stand
in competition with the good of a whole people. It
was upon this principle that I laid it down as a thing
certain, that the African company would be allowed to
settle the island of Madagascar, though it lies within
the limits of the East India Company's charter, in case
it should } s found necessary for the better carrying on

of this trade. It is upon the same principle I say this southern continent lies within the intention of the South Sea Company's charter, because, I presume, the intent of that charter was to grant them all the commerce in those seas, not occupied before by British subjects; for, if it were otherwise, what a condition should we be in as a maritime power? If a grant does not oblige a company to carry on a trade within the limits granted to that company, and is, at the same time, of force to preclude all the subjects of this nation from the right they before had to carry on a trade within those limits, such a law is plainly destructive to the nation's interest and to commerce in general. I therefore suppose, that, if the South Sea Company should think proper to revive their trade in the manner I propose, this proviso would be explained by Parliament to mean no more than excluding the South Sea Company from settling or trading in or to any place at present settled in or traded to by the East India Company: for, as this interpretation would secure the just rights of both companies, and, at the same time, reconcile the laws for establishing them to the general interest of trade and the nation, there is the greatest reason to believe this to be the intention of the legislature. I have been obliged to insist fully upon this matter, because it is a point hitherto untouched, and a point of such high importance, that, unless it be understood according to my sense of the matter, there is an end of all hopes of extending our trade on this side, which is perhaps the only side on which there is the least probability that it ever can be extended; for, as to the north-west passage into the South Seas, that seems to be blocked up by the rights of another company; so that, according to the letter of our laws, each company is to have its rights, and the nation in general no right at all.

If, therefore, the settling of this part of Terra Australis should devolve on the South Sea Company, by way of equivalent for the loss of their Assiento contract, there is no sort of question but it might be as well performed by them as by any other, and the trade carried on without interfering with that which is at present carried on, either by the East India or African Companies. It would indeed, in this case, be absolutely necessary to settle Juan Fernandez, the settlement of which place, under the direction of that company, if they could, as very probably they might, fall into some share of the slave-trade from New Guinea, must prove wonderfully advantageous, considering the opportunity they would have of vending those slaves to the Spaniards in Chili and Peru. The settling of this island ought to be performed at once, and with a competent force, since, without doubt, the Spaniards would leave no means unattempted to dispossess them : yet, if a good fortification was once raised, the passes properly retrenched, and a garrison left there of between three and five hundred men, it would be simply impossible for the Spaniards to force them out of it before the arrival of another squadron from hence. Neither do I see any reason why, in the space of a very few years, the plantation of this island should not prove of as great consequence to the South Sea Company as that of Curacao to the Dutch West India Company, who raise no less than sixty thousand florins per annum for licensing ships to trade there.

From Juan Fernandez to Van Diemen's Land is not above two months' sail; and a voyage for discovery might be very conveniently made between the time that a squadron returned from Juan Fernandez, and another squadron's arrival there from hence. It is true that, if once a considerable settlement was made in the most southern part of Terra Australis, the company might then fall into a large commerce in the most valuable East India goods, very probably gold, and spices of all sorts: yet I cannot think that even these would fall within the exclusive proviso of their charter; for that was certainly intended to hinder their trading in such goods as are brought hither by our East India Company; and I must confess I see no difference, with respect to the interest of that company, between our having cloves, cinnamon, and mace, by the South Sea Company's ships from Juan Fernandez, and our receiving them from Holland, after the Dutch East India Company's ships have brought them thither by the way of the Cape of Good Hope. Sure I am they would come to us sooner by some months by the way of Cape Horn. If this reasoning does not satisfy people, but they still remain persuaded that the South Sea Company ought not to intermeddle with the East India trade at all, I desire to know why the West India merchants are allowed to import coffee from Jamaica, when it is well known that the East India Company can supply the whole demand of this kingdom from Mocha? If it be answered that the Jamaica coffee comes cheaper, and is the growth of our own plantations, I reply, that these spices will not only be cheaper, but better, and be purchased by our own manufacturers; and these, I think, are the strongest reasons that can be given.

If it be demanded what certainty I have that spices can be had from thence, I answer, all the certainty that in a thing of this nature can be reasonably expected: Ferdinand de Quiros met with all sorts of spices in the country he discovered; William Schovten, and Jacques le Maire, saw ginger and nutmegs; so did Dampier; and the author of Commodore Roggewein's Voyage asserts, that the free burgesses of Amboyna purchase nutmegs from the natives of New Guinea for bits of iron. All, therefore, I contend for, is that these bits of iron may be sent them from Old England.

The reason I recommend settling on the south coast of Terra Australis, if this design should be prosecuted, from Juan Fernandez, rather than the island of New Britain, which I mentioned before, is, because that coast is nearer, and is situated in a better and pleasanter

climate.   Besides all which advantages, as it was
never hitherto visited by the Dutch, they cannot, with
any colour of justice, take umbrage at our attempting
such a settlement.   To close then this subject, the importance of which alone inclined me to spend so much
of mine and the reader's time about it:

It is most evident, that, if such a settlement was
made at Juan Fernandez, proper magazines erected,
and a constant correspondence established between
that island and the Terra Australis, these three
consequences must absolutely follow from thence:
1. That a new trade would be opened, which must
carry off a great quantity of our goods and manufactures, that cannot, at present, be brought to any market, or at least, not to so good a market as if there
was a greater demand for them.   2. It would render
this navigation, which is at present so strange, and
consequently so terrible, to us, easy and familiar;
which might be attended with advantages that cannot
be foreseen, especially since there is, as I before observed, in all probability another southern continent,
which is still to be discovered.   3. It would greatly
increase our shipping and our seamen, which are the
true and natural strength of this country, extend our
naval power, and raise the reputation of this nation;
the most distant prospect of which is sufficient to warm
the soul of any man who has the least regard for his
country, with courage sufficient to despise the impu-
tations that may be thrown upon him as a visionary

projector, for taking so much pains about an affair that can tend so little to his private advantage. We will now add a few words with respect to the advantages arising from having thus digested the history of circumnavigators, from the earliest account of time to the present, and then shut up the whole with another section, containing the last circumnavigation by Rear-Admiral Anson, whose voyage has at least shown that, under a proper officer, English seamen are able to achieve as much as they ever did; and that is as much as was ever done by any nation in the world.

It is a point that has always admitted some debate, whether science stands more indebted to speculation or practice; or, in other words, whether the greater discoveries have been made by men of deep study, or persons of great experience in the most useful parts of knowledge. But this, I think, is a proposition that admits of no dispute at all, that the noblest discoveries have been the result of a just mixture of theory with practice. It was from hence that the very notion of sailing round the earth took rise; and the ingenious Genoese first laid down this system of the world, according to his conception, and then added the proofs derived from experience. It is much to be deplored that we have not that plan of discovery which the great Christopher Columbus sent over thither by his brother Bartholomew to King Henry VII., for if we had we should certainly find abundance of very curious observations, which might still be useful to mariners :

for it appears clearly, from many little circumstances, that he was a person of universal genius, and, until bad usage obliged him to take many precautions, very communicative.

It was from this plan, as it had been communicated to the Portuguese court, that the famous Magellan came to have so just notions of the possibility of sailing by the West to the East Indies; and there was a great deal of theory in the proposal made by that great man to the Emperor Charles V. Sir Francis Drake was a person of the same genius, and of a like general knowledge; and it is very remarkable that these three great seamen met also with the same fate; by which I mean, that they were constantly pursued by envy while they lived, which hindered so much notice being taken of their discourses and discoveries as they deserved. But when the experience of succeeding times had verified many of their sayings, which had been considered as vain and empty boastings in their lifetimes, then prosperity began to pay a superstitious regard to whatever could be collected concerning them, and to admire all they delivered as oraculous. Our other discoverer, Candish, was likewise a man of great parts and great penetration, as well as of great spirit; he had, undoubtedly, a mighty genius for discoveries; but the prevailing notion of those times, that the only way to serve the nation was plundering the Spaniards, seems to have got the better of his desire to find out unknown countries; and made

him choose to be known to posterity rather as a gal-
lant privateer than as an able seaman, though in truth
he was both.

After these follow Schovten and Le Maire, who were
fitted out to make discoveries; and executed their commission with equal capacity and success. If Le Maire
had lived to return to Holland, and to have digested
into proper order his own accounts, we should, without
question, have received a much fuller and clearer, as
well as a much more correct and satisfactory detail of
them than we have at present : though the voyage, as
it is now published, is in all respects the best. and the
most curious of all the circumnavigators. This was,
very probably, owing to the ill-usage he met with from
the Dutch East India Company; which put Captain
Schovten, and the relations of Le Maire, upon giving
the world the best information they could of what had
been in that voyage performed. Yet the fate of Le
Maire had a much greater effect in discouraging, than
the fame of his discoveries had in exciting, a spirit of
emulation ; so that we may safely say, the severity of
the East India Company in Holland extinguished that
generous desire of exploring unknown lands, which
might otherwise have raised the reputation and extended the commerce of the republic much beyond what
they have hitherto reached. This is so true that for up-
wards of one hundred years we hear of no Dutch voyage
in pursuit of Le Maire's discoveries; and we see,
when Commodore Roggewein, in our own time, revived

D--43

that noble design, it was again cramped by the same power that stifled it before; and though the States did justice to the West India Company, and to the parties injured, yet the hardships they suffered, and the plain proof they gave of the difficulties that must be met with in the prosecution of such a design, seem to have done the business of the East India Company, and damped the spirit of discovery, for perhaps another century, in Holland.

It is very observable that all the mighty discoveries that have been made arose from these great men, who joined reasoning with practice, and were men of genius and learning, as well as seamen. To Columbus we owe the finding America; to Magellan the passing by the straits which bear his name, by a new route to the East Indies; to Le Maire a more commodious passage round Cape Horn, and without running up to California; Sir Francis Drake, too, hinted the advantages that might arise by examining the north-west side of America; and Candish had some notions of discovering a passage between China and Japan. As to the history we have of Roggewein's voyage, it affords such lights as nothing but our own negligence can render useless. But in the other voyages, whatever discoveries we meet with are purely accidental, except it be Dampier's voyage to the coasts of New Holland and New Guinea, which was expressly made for discoveries; and in which, if an abler man had been employed in conjunction with Dampier, we cannot doubt that the interior and exterior of those countries would have been much better known than they are at present; because such a person would rather have chosen to have refreshed in the Island of New Britain, or some other country not visited before, than at that of Timor, already settled both by the Portuguese and the Dutch.

In all attempts, therefore, of this sort, those men are fittest to be employed who, with competent abilities as seamen, have likewise general capacities, are at least tolerably acquainted with other sciences, and have settled judgments and solid understandings. These are the men from whom we are to expect the finishing that great work which former circumnavigators have begun; I mean the discovering every part and parcel of the globe, and the carrying to its utmost perfection the admirable and useful science of navigation.

It is, however, a piece of justice due to the memory of these great men, to acknowledge that we are equally encouraged by their examples and guided by their discoveries. We owe to them the being freed, not only from the errors, but from the doubts and difficulties with which former ages were oppressed ; to them we stand indebted for the discovery of the best part of the world, which was entirely unknown to the ancients, particularly some part of the eastern, most of the southern, and all the western hemisphere; from them we have learned that the earth is surrounded by the

ocean, and that all the countries under the torrid zone
are inhabited, and that, quite contrary to the notions
that were formerly entertained, they are very far from
being the most sultry climate in the world, those
within a few degrees of the tropics, though habitable,
being much more hot, for reasons which have been
elsewhere explained. By their voyages, and especially
by the observations of Columbus, we have been taught
the general motion of the sea, the reason of it, and the
cause and difference of currents in particular places,
to which we may add the doctrine of tides, which were
very imperfectly known, even by the greatest men in
former times, whose accounts have been found equally
repugnant to reason and experience.

By their observations we have acquired a great
knowledge as to the nature and variation of winds,
particularly the monsoons, or trade winds, and other
periodical winds, of which the ancients had not the
least conception; and by these helps we not only have
it in our power to proceed much farther in our discoveries, but we are likewise delivered from a multi-
tude of groundless apprehensions, that frightened them
from prosecuting discoveries. We give no credit now
to the fables that not only amused antiquity, but even
obtained credit within a few generations. The
authority of Pliny will not persuade us that there are
any nations without heads, whose eyes and mouths are
in their breasts, or that the Arimaspi have only one
eye, fixed in their forehead, and that they are perpetu-

ally at war with the Griffins, who guard hidden
treasures; or that there are nations that have long
hairy tales, and grin like monkeys. No traveller can
make us believe that, under the torrid zone, there are a
nation every man of which has one large flat foot, with
which, lying upon his back, he covers himself from the
sun. In this respect we have the same advantage over
the ancients that men have over children; and we cannot reflect without amazement on men's having so much
knowledge and learning in other respects, with such
childish understandings in these.

By the labours of these great men in the two last
centuries we are taught to know what we seek, and
how it is to be sought. We know, for example, what
parts of the north are yet undiscovered, and also what
parts of the south. We can form a very certain judgment of the climate of countries undiscovered, and can
foresee the advantages that will result from discoveries
before they are made; all which are prodigious advantages, and ought certainly to animate us in our
searches. I might add to this the great benefits we
receive from our more perfect acquaintance with the
properties of the loadstone, and from the surprising
accuracy of astronomical observations, to which I may
add the physical discoveries made of late years in
relation to the figure of the earth, all of which are
the result of the lights which these great men have
given us.

It is true that some of the zealous defenders of the

ancients, and some of the great admirers of the Eastern nations, dispute these facts, and would have us believe that almost everything was known to the old philosophers, and not only known but practised by the Chinese long before the time of the great men to whom we ascribe them. But the difference between their assertions and ours is, that we fully prove the facts we allege, whereas they produce no evidence at all; for instance, Albertus Magnus says that Aristotle wrote an express treatise on the direction of the loadstone; but nobody ever saw that treatise, nor was it ever heard of by any of the rest of his commentators. We have in our hands some of the best performances of antiquity in regard to geography, and any man who has eyes, and is at all acquainted with that science, can very easily discern how far they fall short of maps that were made even a hundred years ago. The celebrated Vossius, and the rest of the admirers of the Chinese, who, by the way, derived all their knowledge from hearsay, may testify, in as strong terms as they think fit, their contempt for the Western sages and their high opinion of those in the East; but till they prove to us that their favourite Chinese made any voyages comparable to the Europeans, before the discovery of a passage to China by the Cape of Good Hope, they will excuse us from believing them. Besides, if the ancients had all this knowledge, how came it not to display itself in their performances? How came they to make such difficulties of what are now esteemed trifles? And how came they never to make any voyages, by choice at least, that were out of sight of land? Again, with respect to the Chinese, if they excel us so much in knowledge, how came the missionaries to be so much admired for their superior skill in the sciences? But to cut the matter short, we are not disputing now about speculative points of science, but as to the practical application of it; in which, I think, there is no doubt that the modern inhabitants of the western parts of the world excel, and excel chiefly from the labours and discoveries of these great and ingenious men, who applied their abilities to the improvement of useful arts, for the particular benefit of their countrymen, and to the common good of mankind; which character is not derived from any prejudice of ours, either against the ancients or the Oriental nations, but is founded on facts of public notoriety, and on general experience, which are a kind of evidence not to be controverted or contradicted.

We are still, however, in several respects short of perfection, and there are many things left to exercise the sagacity, penetration, and application of this and of succeeding ages; for instance, the passages to the north-east and north-west are yet unknown; there is a great part of the southern continent undiscovered; we are, in a manner, ignorant of what lies between America and Japan, and all beyond that country lies buried in obscurity, perhaps in greater obscurity than it was an age ago; so that there is still room for per-

forming great things, which in their consequences
perhaps might prove greater than can well be imagined.
I say nothing of the discoveries that yet remain with
regard to inland countries, because these fall properly
under another head, I mean that of travels.   But it will
be time enough to think of penetrating into the heart of
countries when we have discovered the sea-coasts of
the whole globe, towards which the voyages recorded
in this chapter have so far advanced already.   But the
only means to arrive at these great ends, and to trans-
mit to posterity a fame approaching, at least in some
measure, to that of our ancestors, is to revive and
restore that glorious spirit which led them to such great
exploits ; and the most natural method of doing this is
to collect and preserve the memory of their exploits,
that they may serve at once to excite our imitation,
encourage our endeavours, and point out to us how
they may be best employed, and with the greatest
probability of success.

AN ACCOUNT OF NEW HOLLAND AND THE ADJACENT ISLANDS.

1699—1700.

BY CAPTAIN WILLIAM DAMPIER.

HAVING described his voyago from Brazil to New Holland, this celebrated navigator thus proceeds:

About the latitude of 26° south we saw an opening, and ran in, hoping to find a harbour there ; but when we came to its mouth, which was about two leagues wide, we saw rocks and foul ground within, and therefore stood out again ; there we had twenty fathom water within two miles of the shore : the land everywhere appeared pretty low, flat, and even, but with steep cliffs to the sea, and when we came near it there were no trees, shrubs, or grass to be seen. The soundings in the latitude of 26° south, from about eight or nine leagues off till you come within a league of the shore, are generally about forty fathoms, differing but little, seldom above three or four fathoms ; but the lead brings up very different sorts of sand, some coarse, some fine, and of several colours, as yellow, white, grey, brown, bluish, and reddish.

When I saw there was no harbour here, nor good anchoring, I stood off to sea again in the evening of

the 2nd of August, fearing a storm on a lee-shore, in a
place where there was no shelter, and desiring at least
to have sea-room, for the clouds began to grow thick
in the western-board, and the wind was already there,
and began to blow fresh almost upon the shore, which
at this place lies along north-north-west and south-
south-east. By nine o'clock at night we got a pretty
good offing, but the wind still increasing, I took in my
main-top-sail, being able to carry no more sail than two
courses and the mizen. At two in the morning,
August 3rd, it blew very hard, and the sea was much
raised, so that I furled all my sails but my mainsail,
though the wind blew so hard, we had pretty clear
weather till noon, but then the whole sky was blackened
with thick clouds, and we had some rain, which would
last a quarter of an hour at a time, and then it would
blow very fierce while the squalls of rain were over our
heads, but as soon as they were gone the wind was by
much abated, the stress of the storm being over; we
sounded several times, but had no ground till eight
o'clock, August the 4th, in the evening, and then had
sixty fathom water, coral ground. At ten we had
fifty-six fathom, fine sand. At twelve we had fifty-five
fathom, fine sand, of a pale bluish colour. It was now
pretty moderate weather, yet I made no sail till morning, but then the wind veering about to the south-west,
I made sail and stood to the north, and at eleven o'clock
the next day, August 5th, we saw land again, at about
ten leagues distant. This noon we were in latitude

25° 30', and in the afternoon our cook died, an old man, who had been sick a great while, being infirm before we came out of England.

The 6th of August, in the morning, we saw an opening in the land, and we ran into it, and anchored in seven and a half fathom water, two miles from the shore, clean sand. It was somewhat difficult getting in here, by reason of many shoals we met with; but I sent my boat sounding before me. The mouth of this sound, which I called Shark's Bay, lies in about 25° south latitude, and our reckoning made its longitude from the Cape of Good Hope to be about 87°, which is less by one hundred and ninety-five leagues than is usually laid down in our common draughts, if our reckoning was right and our glasses did not deceive us. As soon as I came to anchor in this bay, I sent my boat ashore to seek for fresh water, but in the evening my men returned, having found none. The next morning I went ashore myself, carrying pickaxes and shovels with me, to dig for water, and axes to cut wood. We tried in several places for water, but finding none after several trials, nor in several miles compass, we left any further search for it, and spending the rest of the day in cutting wood, we went aboard at night.

The land is of an indifferent height, so that it may be seen nine or ten leagues off. It appears at a distance very even; but as you come nigher you find there are many gentle risings, though none steep or high. It is all a steep shore against the open sea; but in this bay

or sound we were now in, the land is low by the seaside,
rising gradually in with the land. The mould is sand
by the seaside, producing a large sort of samphire,
which bears a white flower. Farther in the mould is
reddish, a sort of sand, producing some grass, plants,
and shrubs. The grass grows in great tufts as big as
a bushel, here and there a tuft, being intermixed with
much heath, much of the kind we have growing on our
commons in England. Of trees or shrubs here are
divers sorts, but none above ten feet high, their bodies
about three feet about, and five or six feet high before
you come to the branches, which are bushy, and
composed of small twigs there spreading abroad, though
thick set and full of leaves, which were mostly long
and narrow. The colour of the leaves was on one side
whitish, and on the other green, and the bark of the
trees was generally of the same colour with the leaves,
of a pale green. Some of these trees were sweet-
scented, and reddish within the bark, like sassafras,
but redder. Most of the trees and shrubs had at this
time either blossoms or berries on them. The blossoms
of the different sorts of trees were of several colours,
as red, white, yellow, etc., but mostly blue, and these
generally smelt very sweet and fragrant, as did some
also of the rest. There were also besides some plants,
herbs, and tall flowers, some very small flowers growing
on the ground, that were sweet and beautiful, and, for
the most part, unlike any I had seen elsewhere.

There were but few land fowls. We saw none but

eagles of the larger sorts of birds, but five or six sorts
of small birds. The biggest sort of these were not
bigger than larks, some no bigger than wrens, all
singing with great variety of fine shrill notes; and we
saw some of their nests with young ones in them. The
water-fowls are ducks (which had young ones now, this
being the beginning of the spring in these parts),
curlews, galdens, crab-catchers, cormorants, gulls, pelicans, and some water-fowl, such as I have not seen
anywhere besides.

The land animals that we saw here were only a sort
of raccoons, different from those of the West Indies,
chiefly as to their legs, for these have very short fore-
legs, but go jumping upon them as the others do (and
like them are very good meat), and a sort of guanos, of
the same shape and size with other guanos described,
but differing from them in three remarkable par-
ticulars; for these had a larger and uglier head, and
had no tail, and at the rump, instead of the tail there,
they had a stump of a tail, which appeared like another
head, but not really such, being without mouth or
eyes; yet this creature seemed by this means to have a
head at each end, and, which may be reckoned a fourth
difference, the legs also seemed all four of them to be
fore-legs, being all alike in shape and length, and
seeming by the joints and bending to be made as if
they were to go indifferently either head or tail fore-
most. They were speckled black and yellow like toads,
and had scales or knobs on their backs like those of

crocodiles, plated on to the skin, or stuck into it, as part of the skin. They are very slow in motion, and when a man comes nigh them they will stand still and hiss, not endeavouring to get away. Their livers are also spotted black and yellow; and the body, when opened, hath a very unsavoury smell. I did never see such ugly creatures anywhere but here. The guanos I have observed to be very good meat, and I have often eaten of them with pleasure; but though I have eaten of snakes, crocodiles, and alligators, and many creatures that look frightfully enough, and there are but few I should have been afraid to eat of if pressed by hunger, yet I think my stomach would scarce have served to venture upon these New Holland guanos, both the looks and the smell of them being so offensive.

The sea-fish that we saw here (for here was no river, land or pond of fresh water to be seen) are chiefly sharks. There are abundance of them in this particular sound, that I therefore gave it the name of Shark's Bay. Here are also skates, thornbacks, and other fish of the ray kind (one sort especially like the sea-devil), and gar-fish, bonetas, etc. Of shell-fish we got here mussels, periwinkles, limpets, oysters, both of the pearl kind and also eating oysters, as well the common sort as long oysters, besides cockles, etc. The shore was lined thick with many other sorts of very strange and beautiful shells for variety of colour and shape, most finely spotted with red, black, or yellow, etc., such as I have not seen anywhere but at this place. I brought away a great many of them, but lost all except a very few, and those not of the best.

There are also some green turtle weighing about two hundred pounds. Of these we caught two, which the water ebbing had left behind a ledge of rock which they could not creep over. These served all my company two days, and they were indifferent sweet meat. Of the sharks we caught a great many, which our men ate very savourily. Among them we caught one which was eleven feet long. The space between its two eyes was twenty inches, and eighteen inches from one corner of his mouth to the other. Its maw was like a leather sack, very thick, and so tough that a sharp knife could scarce cut it, in which we found the head and bones of a hippopotamus, the hairy lips of which were still sound and not putrified, and the jaw was also firm, out of which we plucked a great many teeth, two of them eight inches long and as big as a man's thumb, small at one end, and a little crooked, the rest not above half so long. The maw was full of jelly, which stank extremely. However, I saved for awhile the teeth and the shark's jaw. The flesh of it was divided among my men, and they took care that no waste should be made of it.

It was the 7th of August when we came into Shark's Bay, in which we anchored at three several places, and stayed at the first of them (on the west side of the bay) till the 11th, during which time we searched about, as I said, for fresh water, digging wells, but to no purpose. However, we cut good store of firewood at this first anchoring-place, and my company were all here very well refreshed with raccoons, turtle, shark, and other fish, and some fowls, so that we were now all much brisker than when we came in hither. Yet still I was for standing farther into the bay, partly because I had a mind to increase my stock of fresh water, which was begun to be low, and partly for the sake of discovering this part of the coast. I was invited to go further by seeing from this anchoring-place all open before me, which therefore I designed to search before I left the bay. So on the 11th about noon I steered further in, with an easy sail, because we had but shallow water. We kept, therefore, good looking out for fear of shoals, sometimes shortening, sometimes deepening the water. About two in the afternoon we saw the land ahead that makes the south of the bay, and before night we had again sholdings from that shore, and therefore shortened sail and stood off and on all night, under two topsails, continually sounding, having never more than ten fathom, and seldom less than seven. The water deepened and sholdened so very gently, that in heaving the lead five or six times we should scarce have a foot difference. When we came into seven fathom either way, we presently went about. From this south part of the bay we could not see the land from whence we came in the afternoon; and this land we found to be an island of three or four leagues long; but it appearing barren, I did not strive to go nearer it, and the rather because the winds would not permit us to do it without much trouble, and at the openings the water was generally shoal: I therefore made no farther attempts in this south-west and south part of the bay, but steered away to the eastward, to see if there was any land that way, for as yet we had seen none there. On the 12th, in the morning, we passed by the north point of that land, and were confirmed in the persuasion of its being an island by seeing an opening to the east of it, as we had done on the west. Having fair weather, a small gale, and smooth water, we stood further on in the bay to see what land was on the east of it. Our soundings at first were seven fathom, which held so a great while, but at length it decreased to six. Then we saw the land right ahead. We could not come near it with the ship, having but shoal water, and it being dangerous lying there, and the land extraordinarily low, very unlikely to have fresh water (though it had a few trees on it, seemingly mangroves), and much of it probably covered at high water, I stood out again that afternoon, deepening the water, and before night anchored in eight fathom, clean white sand, about the middle of the bay. The next day we got up our anchor, and that afternoon came to an anchor once more near two islands and a shoal of coral rocks that face the bay. Here I scrubbed my ship; and finding it very improbable I should get any further here, I made the best of my way out to sea again, sounding all the way; but finding, by the shallowness of the water, that there was no going out to sea to the east of the two islands that face the bay, nor between them, I returned to the west entrance, going out by the same way I came in at, only on the east instead of the west side of the small shoal: in which channel we had ten, twelve, and thirteen fathom water, still deepening upon us till we were out at sea. The day before we came out I sent a boat ashore to the most northerly of the two islands, which is the least of them, catching many small fish in the meanwhile with hook and line. The boat's crew returning told me that the isle produces nothing but a sort of green, short, hard, prickly grass, affording neither wood nor fresh water, and that a sea broke between the two islands—a sign that the water was shallow. They saw a large turtle, and many skates and thornbacks, but caught none.

It was August the 14th when I sailed out of this bay or sound, the mouth of which lies, as I said, in 25° 5′, designing to coast along to the north-east till I might commodiously put in at some other port of New Holland. In passing out we saw three water-serpents swimming about in the sea, of a yellow colour spotted with dark brown spots. They were each about four foot long, and about the bigness of a man's wrist, and were the first I saw on this coast, which abounds with several sorts of them. We had the winds at our first coming out at north, and the land lying north-easterly. We plied off and on, getting forward but little till the next day, when the wind coming at south-south-west and south, we began to coast it along the shore on the northward, keeping at six or seven leagues off shore, and sounding often, we had between forty and forty-six fathom water, brown sand with some white shells. This 15th of August we were in latitude 24° 41'. On the 16th day, at noon, we were in 23° 22'. The wind coming at east by north, we could not keep the shore aboard, but were forced to go farther off, and lost sight of the land; then sounding, we had no ground with eighty fathom line. However, the wind shortly after came about again to the southward, and then we jogged on again to the northward, and saw many small dolphins and whales, and abundance of cuttle-shells swimming on the sea, and some water-snakes every day. The 17th we saw the land again and took a sight of it.

The 18th, in the afternoon, being three or four leagues off shore, I saw a shoal-point stretching from the land into the sea a league or more; the sea broke high on it, by which I saw plainly there was a shoal there. I stood farther off and coasted along shore to about seven or eight leagues distance, and at twelve o'clock at night we sounded, and had but twenty fathom, hard sand. By this I found I was upon another shoal, and so presently steered off west half an hour, and had then forty fathom. At one in the morning of the 18th day we had eighty-five fathom; by two we could find no ground, and then I ven-

tured to steer along shore again due north, which
is two points wide of the coast (that lies north-north-
east), for fear of another shoal. I would not be too far
off from the land, being desirous to search into it
wherever I should find an opening or any convenience
of searching about for water, etc. When we were off
the shoal-point I mentioned, where we had but twenty
fathom water, we had in the night abundance of whales
about the ship, some ahead, others astern, and some on
each side, blowing and making a very dismal noise; but
when we came out again into deeper water, they left
us; indeed, the noise that they made by blowing and
dashing of the sea with their tails, making it all of a
breach and foam, was very dreadful to us, like the
breach of the waves in very shoal water or among
rocks. The shoal these whales were upon had depth
of water sufficient, no less than twenty fathom, as I
said, and it lies in latitude 22° 22'. The shore was
generally bold all along. We had met with no shoal
at sea since the Abrohlo shoal, when we first fell on
the New Holland coast in the latitude of 28°, till
yesterday in the afternoon and this night. This morning also, when we expected by the draught we had
with us to have been eleven leagues off shore, we were
but four, so that either our draughts were faulty,
which yet hitherto and afterwards we found true
enough as to the lying of the coast, or else here was a
tide unknown to us that deceived us, though we had
found very little of any tide on this coast hitherto; as

to our winds in the coasting thus far, as we had been within the verge of the general trade (though interrupted by the storm I mentioned), from the latitude of 28°, when we first fell in with the coast, and by that time we were in the latitude of 25°, we had usually the regular trade wind (which is here southsouth-east) when we were at any distance from shore; but we had often sea and land breezes, especially when near shore and when in Shark's Bay, and had a particular north-west wind or storm that set us in thither. On this 18th of August we coasted with a brisk gale of the true trade wind at south-south-east, very fair and clear weather; but hauling off in the evening to sea, were next morning out of sight of land, and the land now trending away north-easterly, and we being to the northward of it, and the wind also shrinking from the south-south-east to the east-south-east (that is, from the true trade wind to the sea breeze, as the land now lay), we could not get in with the land again yet awhile so as to see it, though we trimmed sharp and kept close on a wind. We were this 19th day in latitude 21° 42'. The 20th we were in latitude 19° 37', and kept close on a wind to get sight of the land again, but could not yet see it. We had very fair weather, and though we were so far from the land as to be out of sight of it, yet we had the sea and land breezes. In the night we had the land breeze at south-south-east, a small gentle gale, which in the morning about sun-rising would shift about gradually (and withal increasing in strength) till about noon we should have it at east-south-east, which is the true sea breeze here. Then it would blow a brisk gale so that we could scarce carry our top-sails double-reefed; and it would continue thus till three in the afternoon, when it would decrease again. The weather was fair all the while, not a cloud to be seen, but very hazy, especially nigh the horizon. We sounded several times this 20th day, and at first had no ground, but had afterwards from fifty-two to forty-five fathom, coarse brown sand, mixed with small brown and white stones, with dints besides in the tallow.

The 21st day also we had small land breezes in the night, and sea breezes in the day, and as we saw some sea-snakes every day, so this day we saw a great many, of two different sorts or shapes. One sort was yellow, and about the bigness of a man's wrist, about four feet long, having a flat tail about four fingers broad. The other sort was much smaller and shorter, round, and spotted black and yellow. This day we sounded several times, and had forty-five fathom, sand. We did not make the land till noon, and then saw it first from our topmast head; it bore south-east by east about nine leagues distance, and it appeared like a cape or head of land. The sea breeze this day was not so strong as the day before, and it veered out more, so that we had a fair wind to run in with to the shore, and at sunset anchored in twenty fathom, clean sand, about five leagues from the Bluff point, which was not a cape (as it appeared at a great distance), but the easternmost end of an island about five or six leagues in length, and one in breadth. There were three or four rocky islands about a league from us, between us and the Bluff point, and we saw many other islands both to the east and west of it, as far as we could see either way from our topmast-head, and all within them to the south there was nothing but islands of a pretty height, that may be seen eight or nine leagues off; by what we saw of them they must have been a range of islands of about twenty leagues in length, stretching from east-north-east to west-south-west, and, for aught I know, as far as to those of Shark's Bay, and to a considerable breadth also, for we could see nine or ten leagues in among them, towards the continent or mainland of New Holland, if there be any such thing hereabouts; and by the great tides I met with awhile afterwards, more to the north-east, I had a strong suspicion that here might be a kind of archipelago of islands, and a passage possibly to the south of New Holland and New Guinea into the great South Sea eastward, which I had thoughts also of attempting in my return from New Guinea, had circumstances permitted, and told my officers so; but I would not attempt it at this time, because we wanted water, and could not depend upon finding it there. This place is in the latitude of 20° 21', but in the draught that I had of this coast, which was Tasman's, it was laid down in 19° 50', and the shore is laid down as all along joining in one body or continent, with some openings appearing like rivers, and not like islands as really they are. This place lies more northerly by 40' than is laid down in Mr. Tasman's draught, and besides its being made a firm continued land, only with some openings like the mouths of rivers, I found the soundings also different from what the pricked line of his course shows them, and generally shallower than he makes them, which inclines me to think that he came not so near the shore as his line shows, and so had deeper soundings, and could not so well distinguish the islands. His meridian or difference of longitude from Shark's Bay agrees well enough with my account, which is two hundred and thirty-two leagues, though we differ in latitude; and to confirm my conjecture that the line of his course is made too near the shore, at least not far to the east of this place, the water is there so shallow that he could not come there so nigh.

But to proceed. In the night we had a small land breeze, and in the morning I weighed anchor, designing to run in among the islands, for they had large channels between them of a league wide at least, and some two or three leagues wide. I sent in my boat before to sound, and if they found shoal water to return again, but if they found water enough to go ashore on one of the islands and stay till the ship came in, where they might in the meantime search for water. So we followed after with the ship, sounding as we

went in, and had twenty fathom till within two leagues
of the Bluff head, and then we had shoal water and
very uncertain soundings; yet we ran in still with an
easy sail, sounding and looking out well, for this was
dangerous work. When we came abreast of the Bluff
head, and about two miles from it, we had but seven
fathom, then we edged away from it, but had no more
water, and running in a little farther we had but four
fathoms, so we anchored immediately; and yet when
we had veered out a third of a cable, we had seven
fathom water again, so uncertain was the water. My
boat came immediately on board, and told me that the
island was very rocky and dry, and they had little
hopes of finding water there. I sent them to sound,
and bade them, if they found a channel of eight or ten
fathom water, to keep on, and we would follow with
the ship. We were now about four leagues within the
outer small rocky islands, but still could see nothing
but islands within us, some five or six leagues long,
others not above a mile round. The large islands were
pretty high, but all appeared dry, and mostly rocky and
barren. The rocks looked of a rusty yellow colour,
and therefore I despaired of getting water on any of
them, but was in some hopes of finding a channel to
run in beyond all these islands, could I have spent
time here, and either got to the main of New Holland
or find out some other islands that might afford us
water and other refreshments; besides that among so
many islands we might have found some sort of rich

mineral, or ambergris, it being a good latitude for both these. But we had not sailed above a league farther before our water grew shoaler again, and then we anchored in six fathom, hard sand.

We were now on the inner side of the island, on whose outside is the Bluff point. We rode a league from the island, and I presently went ashore and carried shovels to dig for water, but found none. There grow here two or three sorts of shrubs, one just like rosemary, and therefore I called this Rosemary Island; it grew in great plenty here, but had no smell. Some of the other shrubs had blue and yellow flowers; and we found two sorts of grain like beans; the one grew on bushes, the other on a sort of creeping vine that runs along on the ground, having very thick broad leaves, and the blossom like a bean blossom, but much larger and of a deep red colour, looking very beautiful. We saw here some cormorants, gulls, crab-catchers, etc., a few small land birds, and a sort of white parrots, which flew a great many together. We found some shell-fish, viz., limpets, periwinkles, and abundance of small oysters growing on the rocks, which were very sweet. In the sea we saw some green turtle, many sharks, and abundance of water-snakes of several sorts and sizes. The stones were all of rusty colour, and ponderous.

We saw a smoke on an island three or four leagues off, and here also the bushes had been burned, but we found no other sign of inhabitants. It was probable

that on the island where the smoke was there were inhabitants, and fresh water for them. In the evening I
went aboard, and consulted with my officers whether it
was best to send thither, or to search among any other
of these islands with my boat, or else go from hence
and coast along shore with the ship, till we could find
some better place than this was to ride in, where we
had shoal water and lay exposed to winds and tides.
They all agreed to go from hence, so I gave orders to
weigh in the morning as soon as it should be light, and
to get out with the land breeze.

Accordingly, August 23rd, at five in the morning,
we ran out, having a pretty fresh land breeze at south-
south-east. By eight o'clock we were got out, and
very seasonably, for before nine the sea breeze came on
us very strong, and increasing, we took in our top-sails
and stood off under two courses and a mizen, this being
as much sail as we could carry. The sky was clear,
there being not one cloud to be seen, but the horizon
appeared very hazy, and the sun at setting the night
before, and this morning at rising, appeared very red.
The wind continued very strong till twelve, then it
began to abate; I have seldom met with a stronger
breeze. These strong sea breezes lasted thus in their
turns three or four days. They sprang up with the
sunrise; by nine o'clock they were very strong, and
so continued till noon, when they began to abate; and
by sunset there was little wind, or a calm, till the land
breezes came, which we should certainly have in the

morning about one or two o'clock. The land breezes were between the south-south-west and south-south-east: the sea breezes between the east-north-east and north-north-east. In the night while calm, we fished with hook and line, and caught good store of fish, viz., snappers, breams, old-wives, and dog-fish. When these last came we seldom caught any others; for if they did not drive away the other fish, yet they would be sure to keep them from taking our hooks, for they would first have them themselves, biting very greedily. We caught also a monk-fish, of which I brought home the picture.

On the 25th of August we still coasted along shore, that we might the better see any opening; kept sounding, and had about twenty fathom, clean sand. The 26th day, being about four leagues off shore, the water began gradually to sholden from twenty to fourteen fathom. I was edging in a little towards the land, thinking to have anchored; but presently after the water decreased almost at once, till we had but five fathom. I durst, therefore, adventure no farther, but steered out the same way that we came in, and in a short time had ten fathom (being then about four leagues and a half from the shore), and even soundings. I steered away east-north-east, coasting along as the land lies. This day the sea breezes began to be very moderate again, and we made the best of our way along shore, only in the night edging off a little for fear of shoals. Ever since we left Shark's

Bay we had fair clear weather, and so for a great while still.

The 27th day we had twenty fathom water all night, yet we could not see land till one in the afternoon from our topmast-head. By three we could just discern land from our quarter-deck; we had then sixteen fathom. The wind was at north, and we steered east-by-north, which is but one point in on the land; yet we decreased our water very fast, for at four we had but nine fathom, the next cast but seven, which frightened us; and we then tacked instantly and stood off, but in a short time the wind coming at north-west and west-north-west, we tacked again and steered north-north-east, and then deepened our water again, and had all night from fifteen to twenty fathom.

The 28th day we had between twenty and forty fathom. We saw no land this day, but saw a great many snakes and some whales. We saw also some boobies and noddy-birds, and in the night caught one of these last. It was of another shape and colour than any I had seen before. It had a small long bill, as all of them have, flat feet like ducks' feet, its tail forked like a swallow, but longer and broader, and the fork deeper than that of the swallow, with very long wings; the top or crown of the head of this noddy was coal-black, having also small black streaks round about and close to the eyes; and round these streaks on each side, a pretty broad white circle. The breast, belly, and under part of the wings of this noddy were white, and the back and upper part of its wings of a faint black or smoke colour. Noddies are seen in most places between the tropics, as well in the East Indies and on the coast of Brazil, as in the West Indies. They rest ashore at night, and therefore we never see them far at sea, not above twenty or thirty leagues, unless driven off in a storm. When they come about a ship they commonly perch in the night, and will sit still till they are taken by the seamen. They build on cliffs against the sea, or rocks.

The 30th day, being in latitude 18° 21', we made the land again, and saw many great smokes near the shore; and having fair weather and moderate breezes, I steered in towards it. At four in the afternoon I anchored in eight fathom water, clear sand, about three leagues and a half from the shore. I presently sent my boat to sound nearer in, and they found ten fathom about a mile farther in, and from thence still farther in the water decreased gradually to nine, eight, seven, and at two miles distance to six fathom. This evening we saw an eclipse of the moon, but it was abating before the moon appeared to us; for the horizon was very hazy, so that we could not see the moon till she had been half an hour above the horizon; and at two hours twenty-two minutes after sunset, by the reckoning of our glasses, the eclipse was quite gone, which was not of many digits. The moon's centre was then 33° 40' high.

The 31st of August, betimes in the morning, I went

ashore with ten or eleven men to search for water. We went armed with muskets and cutlasses for our defence, expecting to see people there, and carried also shovels and pickaxes to dig wells. When we came near the shore we saw three tall, black, naked men on the sandy bay ahead of us; but as we rowed in, they went away. When we were landed, I sent the boat with two men in her to lie a little from the shore at an anchor, to prevent being seized; while the rest of us went after the three black men, who were now got on the top of a small hill about a quarter of a mile from us, with eight or nine men more in their company. They, seeing us coming, ran away. When we came on the top of the hill where they first stood, we saw a plain savannah, about half a mile from us, farther in from the sea. There were several things like hay-cocks standing in the savannah, which at a distance we thought were houses, looking just like the Hottentots' houses at the Cape of Good Hope: but we found them to be so many rocks. We searched about these for water, but could find none, nor any houses, nor people, for they were all gone. Then we turned again to the place where we landed, and there we dug for water.

While we were at work there came nine or ten of the natives to a small hill a little way from us, and stood there menacing and threatening us, and making a great noise. At last one of them came towards us, and the rest followed at a distance. I went out to meet him, and came within fifty yards of him, making to him all the signs of peace and friend-ship I could, but then he ran away, neither would they any of them stay for us to come nigh them, for we tried two or three times. At last I took two men with me, and went in the afternoon along by the sea-side, purposely to catch one of them, if I could, of whom I might learn where they got their fresh water. There were ten or twelve of the natives a little way off, who, seeing us three going away from the rest of our men, followed us at a distance. I thought they would follow us, but there being for awhile a sand-bank between us and them, that they could not then see us, we made a halt, and hid ourselves in a bending of the sand-bank. They knew we must be thereabouts, and being three or four times our numbers, thought to seize us. So they dispersed themselves, some going to the sea-shore, and others beating about the sand-hills. We knew by what rencounter we had had with them in the morning that we could easily out-run them, so a nimble young man that was with me, seeing some of them near, ran towards them; and they for some time ran away before him, but he soon overtaking them, they faced about and fought him. He had a cutlass and they had wooden lances, with which, being many of them, they were too hard for him. When he first ran towards them I chased two more that were by the shore; but fearing how it might be with my young man, I turned back quickly and went to the top of a sand-hill, whence I saw him near me, closely engaged with them. Upon their seeing me, one of them threw a lance at me, that narrowly missed me. I discharged my gun to scare them, but avoided shooting any of them, till finding the young man in great danger from them, and myself in some; and that though the gun had a little frightened them at first, yet they had soon learnt to despise it, tossing up their hands and crying, "pooh, pooh, pooh," and coming on afresh with a great noise, I thought it high time to charge again, and shoot one of them, which I did. The rest, seeing him fall, made a stand again, and my young man took the opportunity to disengage himself and come off to me; my other man also was with me, who had done nothing all this while, having come out unarmed, and I returned back with my men, designing to attempt the natives no farther, being very sorry for what had happened already. They took up their wounded companion; and my young man, who had been struck through the cheek by one of their lances, was afraid it had been poisoned, but I did not think that likely. His wound was very painful to him, being made with a blunt weapon; but he soon recovered of it.

Among the New Hollanders, whom we were thus engaged with, there was one who by his appearance and carriage, as well in the morning as this afternoon, seemed to be the chief of them, and a kind of prince or captain among them. He was a young brisk man, not very tall, nor so personable as some of the rest,

E—43

though more active and courageous: he was painted
(which none of the rest were at all) with a circle of
white paste or pigment (a sort of lime, as we thought
about his eyes, and a white streak down his nose, from
his forehead to the tip of it : and his breast and some
part of his arms were also made white with the same
paint; not for beauty or ornament, one would think,
but as some wild Indian warriors are said to do, he
seemed thereby to design the looking more terrible:
this his painting adding very much to his natural
deformity; for they all of them have the most un-
pleasant looks and the worst features of any people
that ever I saw, though I have seen great variety of
savages. These New Hollanders were probably the same
sort of people as those I met with on this coast in my
voyage round the world, for the place I then touched
at was not above forty or fifty leagues to the north-east
of this, and these were much the same blinking
creatures (here being also abundance of the same kind
of flesh-flies teazing them,) and with the same black
skins, and hair frizzled, tall and thin, &c. as those
were : but we had not the opportunity to see whether
these, as the former, wanted two of their fore-teeth.

We saw a great many places where they had made
fires, and where there were commonly three or four
boughs stuck up to windward of them ; for the wind,
(which is the sea-breeze), in the day-time blows always
one way with them, and the land-breeze is but small.
By their fire-places we should always find great heaps

of fish-shells of several sorts; and it is probable that theso poor creatures hero lived chiefly on the shell-fish, as those I before described did on small fish, which they caught in wires or holes in the sand at low water. These gathered their shell-fish on the rocks at low water but had no wires (that we saw), whereby to get any other sorts of fish; as among the former I saw not any heaps of shells as here, though I know they also gathered some shell-fish. The lances also of those were such as these had; however, they being upon an island, with their women and children, and all in our power, they did not there use them against us, as here on the continent, where we saw none but some of the men under head, who come out purposely to observe us. We saw no houses at either place, and I believe they have none, since tho former people on the island had none, though they had all their families with them.

Upon returning to my men I saw that though they had dug eight or nine feet deep, yet found no water. So I returned aboard that evening, and the next day, being September 1st, I sent my boatswain ashore to dig deeper, and sent the seine with him to catch fish. While I stayed aboard I observed the flowing of the tide, which runs very swift here, so that our nun-buoy would not bear above the water to be seen. It flows here (as on that part of New Holland I described formerly) about five fathom; and here the flood runs south-east by south till the last quarter; then it sets right in towards the shore (which lies here south-south-west and north-north-east) and the ebb runs north-west by north. When the tides slackened we fished with hook and line, as we had already done in several places on this coast; on which in this voyage hitherto we had found but little tides; but by the height, and strength. and course of them hereabouts, it should seem that if there be such a passage or strait going through eastward to the great South Sea, as I said one might suspect, one would expect to find the mouth of it somewhere between this place and Rosemary Island, which was the part of New Holland I came last from.

Next morning my men came aboard and brought a runlet of brackish water which they had got out of another well that they dug in a place a mile off, and about half as far from the shore; but this water was not fit to drink. However, we all concluded that it would serve to boil our oatmeal, for burgoo, whereby we might save the remains of our other water for drinking, till we should get more : and accordingly the next day we brought aboard four hogsheads of it : but while we were at work about the well we were sadly pestered with the flies, which were more troublesome to us than the sun, though it shone clear and strong upon us all the while very hot. All this while we saw no more of the natives, but saw some of the smoke of some of their fires at two or three miles distance.

The land hereabouts was much like the port of New Holland that I formerly described; it is low, but seemingly barricaded with a long chain of sand-hills to the sea, that lets nothing be seen of what is farther within land. At high water the tides rising so high as they do, the coast shows very low : but when it is low water it seems to be of an indifferent height. At low water-mark the shore is all rocky, so that then there is no landing with a boat ; but at high water a boat may come in over those rocks to the sandy bay, which runs all along on this coast. The land by the sea for about five or six hundred yards is a dry sandy soil, bearing only shrubs and bushes of divers sorts. Some of these had them at this time of the year, yellow flowers or blossoms, some blue, and some white; most of them of a very fragrant smell. Some had fruit like peascods, in each of which there were just ten small peas ; I opened many of them, and found no more nor less. There are also here some of that sort of bean which I saw at Rosemary Island : and another sort of small red hard pulse, growing in cods also, with little black eyes like beans. I know not their names, but have seen them used often in the East Indies for weighing gold; and they make the same use of them at Guinea, as I have heard, where the women also make bracelets with them to wear about their arms. These grow on bushes ; but here are also a fruit like beans growing on a creeping sort of shrub-like vine. There was great plenty of all these sorts of cod-fruit growing on the sand-hills by the sea side, some of them green, some ripe, and some fallen on the ground :

but I could not perceive that any of them had been gathered by the natives; and might not probably be wholesome food.

The land farther in, that is, lower than what borders on the sea, was so much as we saw of it, very plain and even; partly savannahs and partly woodland. The savannahs bear a sort of thin coarse grass. The mould is also a coarser sand than that by the sea-side, and in some places it is clay. Here are a great many rocks in the large savannah we were in, which are five or six feet high, and round at top like a hay-cock, very remarkable; some red and some white. The woodland lies farther in still, where there were divers sorts of small trees, scarce any three feet in circumference, their bodies twelve or fourteen feet high, with a head of small knibs or boughs. By the sides of the creeks, especially nigh the sea, there grow a few small black mangrove-trees.

There are but few land animals. I saw some lizards; and my men saw two or three beasts like hungry wolves, lean like so many skeletons, being nothing but skin and bones; it is probable that it was the foot of one of those beasts that I mentioned as seen by us in New Holland. We saw a raccoon or two, and one small speckled snake.

The land fowls that we saw here were crows, just such as ours in England, small hawks and kites, a few of each sort: but here are plenty of small turtle doves, that are plump, fat, and very good meat. Here are two or three sorts of smaller birds, some as big as larks, some less; but not many of either sort. The sea-fowl are pelicans, boobies, noddies, curlews, sea-pies, &c., and but few of these neither.

The sea is plentifully stocked with the largest whales that I ever saw ; but not to compare with the vast ones of the Northern Seas. We saw also a great many green turtle, but caught none, here being no place to set a turtle net in; there being no channel for them, and the tides running so strong. We saw some sharks and parracoots; and with hooks and lines we caught some rock-fish and old-wives. Of shell-fish, here were oysters both of the common kind for eating, and of the pearl kind; and also whelks, conchs, muscles, limpits, periwinkles, &c., and I gathered a few strange shells, chiefly a sort not large, and thick-set all about with rays or spikes growing in rows.

And thus having ranged about a considerable time upon this coast, without finding any good fresh water or any convenient place to clean the ship, as I had hoped for; and it being moreover the height of the dry season, and my men growing scorbutic for want of refreshments, so that I had little encouragement to search further, I resolved to leave this coast, and accordingly in the beginning of September set sail towards Timor.

On the 12th of December, 1699, we sailed from Babao, coasting along the island Timor to the eastward, towards New Guinea. It was the 20th before we got as far as Laphao, which is but forty leagues. We saw black clouds in the north-west, and expected the wind from that quarter above a month sooner.

That afternoon we saw the opening between the islands Omba and Fetter, but feared to pass through in the night. At two o'clock in the morning it fell calm, and continued so till noon, in which time we drove with the current back again south-west six or seven leagues.

On the 22nd, steering to the eastward to get through between Omba and Fetter, we met a very strong tide against us, so that although we had a very fresh gale, we yet made way very slowly; but before night got through. By a good observation we found that the south-east point of Omba lies in latitude 8° 25'. In my drafts it is laid down in 8° 10'. My true course from Babao, is east 25° north, distance one hundred eighty-three miles. We sounded several times when near Omba, but had no ground. On the north-east point of Omba we saw four or five men, and a little further three pretty houses on a low point, but did not go ashore.

At five this afternoon we had a tornado, which yielded much rain, thunder, and lightning; yet we had but little wind. The 24th in the morning we caught a large shark, which gave all the ship's company a plentiful meal.

The 27th we saw the Burning Island; it lies in latitude 6° 36' south; it is high, and but small; it runs from the sea a little sloping towards the top, which is divided in the middle into two peaks, between which issued out much smoke : I have not seen more from any volcano. I saw no trees ; but the north side appeared green, and the rest looked very barren.

Having passed the Burning Island, I shaped my course for two islands, called Turtle Isles, which lie north-east by east a little easterly, and distant about fifty leagues from the Burning Isle. I fearing the wind might veer to the eastward of the north, steered twenty leagues north-east, then north-east by east. On the 28th we saw two small low islands, called Lucea-Parros, to the north of us. At noon I accounted myself twenty leagues short of the Turtle Isles.

The next morning, being in the latitude of the Turtle Islands, we looked out sharp for them, but saw no appearance of any island till eleven o'clock, when we saw an island at a great distance. At first we supposed it might be one of the Turtle Isles, but it was not laid down true, neither in latitude nor longitude from the Burning Isle, nor from the Lucea-Parros, which last I took to be a great help to guide me, they being laid down very well from the Burning Isle, and that likewise in true latitude and distance from Omba, so that I could not tell what to think of the island now in sight, we having had fair weather, so that we could not pass by the Turtle Isles without seeing them, and this in sight was much too far off for them. We found variation 1° 2′ east. In the afternoon I steered north-east by east for the islands that we saw. At two o'clock I went and looked over the fore-yard, and saw two islands at much greater distance than the Turtle Islands are laid down in my drafts, one of them was a very high peaked mountain, cleft at top, and much like the Burning Island that we passed by, but bigger and higher; the other was a pretty long high flat island. Now I was certain that these were not the Turtle Islands, and that they could be no other than the Bande Isles, yet we steered in to make them plainer. At three o'clock we discovered another small flat island to the north-west of the others, and saw a great deal of smoke rise from the top of the high island. At four we saw other small islands, by which I was now assured that these were the Bande Isles there. At five I altered my course and steered east, and at eight east-south-east, because I would not be seen by the in-habitants of those islands in the morning. We had little wind all night, and in the morning, as soon as it was light we saw another high peaked island; at eight it bore south-south-east half-east, distance eight leagues: and this I knew to be Bird Isle. It is laid down in our drafts in latitude 5° 9' south, which is too far southerly by twenty-seven miles, according to our observation, and the like error in laying down the Turtle Islands might be the occasion of our missing them.

At night I shortened sail, for fear of coming too nigh some islands, that stretch away bending like a half moon from Ceram towards Timor, and which in

my course I must of necessity pass through. The
next morning betimes I saw them, and found them to
be at a farther distance from Bird Island than I expected.   In the afternoon it fell quite calm, and
when we had a little wind, it was so unconstant, flying
from one point to another, that I could not without
difficulty get through the islands where I designed;
besides, I found a current setting to the southward, so
that it was betwixt five and six in the evening before I
passed through the islands, and then just weathered
little Watela, whereas I thought to have been two
or three leagues more northerly.   We saw the day
before, betwixt two and three, a spout but a small distance from us, it fell down out of a black cloud, that
yielded great store of rain, thunder and lightning;
this cloud hovered to the southward of us for the space
of three hours, and then drew to the westward a great
pace, at which time it was that we saw the spout, which
hung fast to the cloud till it broke, and then the cloud
whirled about to the south-east, then to east-north-
east, where meeting with an island, it spent itself and
so dispersed, and immediately we had a little of the
tail of it, having had none before.   Afterwards we saw
a smoke on the island Kosiway, which continued till
night.

On New Year's Day we first descried the land of
New Guinea, which appeared to be high land, and the
next day we saw several high islands on the coast of
New Guinea, and ran in with the main land. The shore

here lies along east-south-east and west-north-west. It is high even land, very well clothed with tall flourishing trees, which appeared very green, and gave us a very pleasant prospect. We ran to the westward of four mountainous islands, and in the night had a small tornado, which brought with it some rain and a fair wind. We had fair weather for a long time, only when near any land we had some tornadoes; but off, at sea, commonly clear weather, though, if in sight of land, we usually saw many black clouds hovering about it.

On the 5th and 6th of January we plied to get in with the land, designing to anchor, fill water, and spend a little time in searching the country, till after the change of the moon, for I found a strong current setting against us. We anchored in thirty-eight fathom water, good oozy ground. We had an island of a league long without us, about three miles distant, and we rode from the main about a mile. The easternmost point of land seen bore east-by-south half-south, distance three leagues, and the westernmost west-south-west half-south, distance two leagues. So soon as we anchored, we sent the pinnace to look for water and try if they could catch any fish. Afterwards we sent the yawl another way to see for water. Before night the pinnace brought on board several sorts of fruits that they found in the woods, such as I never saw before. One of my men killed a stately land-fowl, as big as the largest dunghill cock; it was of a sky-colour, only in the middle of the wings was a white spot, about which were some reddish spots; on the crown it had a large bunch of long feathers, which appeared very pretty; his bill was like a pigeon's; he had strong legs and feet, like dunghill fowls, only the claws were reddish; his crop was full of small berries. It lays an egg as big as a large hen's egg, for our men climbed the tree where it nested, and brought off one egg. They found water, and reported that the trees were large, tall, and very thick, and that they saw no sign of people. At night the yawl came aboard and brought a wooden fish-spear, very ingeniously made, the matter of it was a small cane; they found it by a small barbecue, where they also saw a shattered canoe.

The next morning I sent the boatswain ashore fishing, and at one haul he caught three hundred and fifty-two mackerel, and about twenty other fishes, which I caused to be equally divided among all my company. I sent also the gunner and chief mate to search about if they could find convenient anchoring near a watering-place; by night they brought word that they had found a fine stream of good water, where the boat could come close to, and it was very easy to be filled, and that the ship might anchor as near to it as I pleased, so I went thither. The next morning, therefore, we anchored in twenty-five fathom water, soft oozy ground, about a mile from the river; we got on board three tuns of water that night, and caught two or three pike-fish, in shape much like a parracota, but with a longer snout, something resembling a garr, yet not so long. The next day I sent the boat again for water, and before night all my casks were full.

Having filled here about fifteen tuns of water, seeing we could catch but little fish, and had no other refreshments, I intended to sail next day, but finding that we wanted wood, I sent to cut some, and going ashore to hasten it, at some distance from the place where our men were, I found a small cove, where I saw two barbecues, which appeared not to be above two months' standing; the spars were cut with some sharp instrument, so that, if done by the natives, it seems that they have iron. On the 10th, a little after twelve o'clock, we weighed and stood over to the north side of the bay, and at one o'clock stood out with the wind at north and north-north-west. At four we passed out by a White Island, which I so named from its many white cliffs, having no name in our drafts. It is about a league long, pretty high, and very woody; it is about five miles from the main, only at the west end it reaches within three miles of it. At some distance off at sea the west point appears like a cape-land, the north side trends away north-north-west, and the east side east-south-east. This island lies in latitude 3° 4' south, and the meridian distance from Babao five hundred and twelve miles east. After we were out to sea, we plied to get to the northward, but met with such a strong current against us, that we got but little, for if the wind favoured us in the night, that we got three or four leagues, we lost it again, and were driven as far astern next morning, so that we plied here several days.

The 14th, being past a point of land that we had been three days getting about, we found little or no current, so that, having the wind at north-west-by-west and west-north-west, we stood to the northward, and had several soundings : at three o'clock thirty-eight fathom, the nearest part of New Guinea being about three leagues' distance ; at four, thirty-seven ; at five, thirty-six ; at six, thirty-six ; at eight, thirty-three fathom ; then the Cape was about four leagues' distant, so that as we ran off we found our water shallower ; we had then some islands to the westward of us, at about four leagues' distance.

A little after noon we saw smoke on the islands to the west of us, and having a fine gale of wind, I steered away for them. At seven o'clock in the evening we anchored in thirty-five fathom, about two leagues from an island, good soft oozy ground. We lay still all night, and saw fires ashore. In the morning we weighed again, and ran farther in, thinking to have shallower water; but we ran within a mile of the shore, and came to in thirty-eight fathom good soft holding ground. While we were under sail two canoes came off within call of us. They spoke to us, but we did not understand their language nor signs. We waved to them to come aboard, and I called to them in the Malayan language to do the same, but they would not. Yet they

came so nigh us that we could show them such things
as we had to truck with them; yet neither would this
entice them to come on board, but they made signs for
us to come ashore, and away they went. Then I went
after them in my pinnace, carrying with me knives,
beads, glasses, hatchets, &c. When we came near the
shore, I called to them in the Malayan language. I saw
but two men at first, the rest lying in ambush behind
the bushes; but as soon as I threw ashore some knives
and other toys, they came out, flung down their
weapons, and came into the water by the boat's side,
making signs of friendship by pouring water on their
heads with one hand, which they dipped into the sea.
The next day, in the afternoon, several other canoes
came aboard, and brought many roots and fruits, which
we purchased.

The island has no name in our drafts, but the natives
call it Pulo Sabuda; it is about three leagues long, and
two miles wide, more or less; it is of a good height, so
as to be seen eleven or twelve leagues; it is very rocky,
yet above the rocks there is good yellow and black
mould, not deep, yet producing plenty of good tall
trees, and bearing any fruits or roots which the inhabitants plant. I do not know all its produce, but
what we saw were plantains, cocoa-nuts, pine-apples,
oranges, papaes, potatoes, and other large roots. Here
are also another sort of wild jacas, about the bigness of
a man's two fists, full of stones or kernels, which eat
pleasant enough when roasted. The libby tree grows

here in the swampy valleys, of which they make sago cakes. I did not see them make any, but was told by the inhabitants that it was made of the pith of the tree, in the same manner I have described in my "Voyage Round the World." They showed me the tree whereof it was made, and I bought about forty of the cakes. I bought also three or four nutmegs in their shell, which did not seem to have been long gathered; but whether they be the growth of this island or not, the natives would not tell whence they had them, and seem to prize them very much. What beasts the island affords I know not, but here are both sea and land fowl. Of the first, boobies and men-of-war birds are the chief, some goldens, and small milk-white crab-catchers; the land-fowl are pigeons, about the bigness of mountain-pigeons in Jamaica, and crows about the bigness of those in England, and much like them, but the inner part of their feathers are white, and the outside black, so that they appear all black, unless you extend the feathers. Here are large sky-coloured birds, such as we lately killed on New Guinea, and many other small birds, unknown to us. Here are likewise abundance of bats, as big as young coneys, their necks, head, ears, and noses like foxes, their hair rough, that about their necks is of a whitish yellow, that on their heads and shoulders black, their wings are four feet over from tip to tip; they smell like foxes. The fish are bass, rock-fish, and a sort of fish like mullets, old-wives, whip-rays, and some other sorts that I know not;

but no great plenty of any, for it is deep water till within less than a mile of the shore, then there is a bank of coral rocks, within which you have shoal-water, white clean sand, so there is no good fishing with the seine.

This island lies in latitude 2° 43' south, and meridian distance from port Babo, on the island Timor, four hundred and eighty-six miles: besides this island, here are nine or ten other small islands.

The inhabitants of this island are a sort of very tawny Indians, with long black hair, who in their manners differ but little from the Mindanayans, and others of these eastern islands. These seem to be the chief; for besides them we saw also shock curl pated New Guinea negroes, many of which are slaves to the others, but I think not all. They are very poor, wear no clothes but have a clout about their middle, made of the rinds of the tops of palmetto trees; but the women had a sort of calico cloth. Their chief ornaments are blue and yellow beads, worn about their wrists. The men arm themselves with bows and arrows, lances, broad swords, like those of Mindanao; their lances are pointed with bone: they strike fish very ingeniously with wooden fish-spears, and have a very ingenious way of making the fish rise; for they have a piece of wood curiously carved, and painted much like a dolphin (and perhaps other figures); these they let down into the water by a line with a small weight to sink it; when they think it low enough, they haul the line into their boats very fast, and the fish rise up after this figure, and they stand ready to strike them when they are near the surface of the water. But their chief livelihood is from their plantations; yet they have large boats, and go over to New Guinea, where they get slaves, fine parrots, &c., which they carry to Goram and exchange for calicoes. One boat came from thence a little before I arrived here, of whom I bought some parrots, and would have bought a slave but they would not barter for anything but calicoes, which I had not. Their houses on this side were very small, and seemed only to be for necessity; but on the other side of the island we saw good large houses. Their prows are narrow, with outriggers on each side, like other Malayans.' I cannot tell of what religion these are; but I think they are not Mahometans, by their drinking brandy out of the same cup with us without any scruple. At this island we continued till the 20th instant, having laid in store of such roots and fruits as the island afforded.

On the 20th, at half an hour after six in the morning, I weighed, and standing out we saw a large boat full of men lying at the north point of the island. As we passed by, they rowed towards their habitations, where we supposed they had withdrawn themselves for fear of us, though we gave them no cause of terror, or for some differences among themselves.

We stood to the northward till seven in the evening, then saw a rippling; and, the water being discoloured, we sounded, and had but twenty-two fathom. I went about and stood to the westward till two next morning, then tacked again, and had these several soundings : at eight in the evening, twenty-two; at ten, twenty-five ; at eleven, twenty-seven; at twelve, twenty-eight fathom; at two in the morning, twenty-six ; at four, twenty-four ; at six, twenty-three; at eight, twenty-eight ; at twelve, twenty-two.

We passed by many small islands, and among many dangerous shoals without any remarkable occurrence till the 4th of February, when we got within three leagues of the north-west cape of New Guinea, called by the Dutch Cape Mabo. Off this cape there lies a small woody island, and many islands of different sizes to the north and north-east of it. This part of New Guinea is high land, adorned with tall trees, that appeared very green and flourishing. The cape itself is not very high, but ends in a low sharp point, and on either side there appears another such point at equal distances, which makes it resemble a diamond. This only appears when you are abreast of the middle point, and then you have no ground within three leagues of the shore.

In the afternoon we passed by the cape and stood over for the islands. Before it was dark we were got within a league of the westernmost, but had no ground with fifty fathom of line : however, fearing to stand nearer in the dark, we tacked and stood to the east, and plied all night. The next morning we were got five or six leagues to the eastward of that island, and, having the wind easterly, we stood in to the northward among the islands, sounded, and had no ground; then I sent in my boat to sound, and they had ground with fifty fathom near a mile from the shore. We tacked before the boat came aboard again, for fear of a shoal that was about a mile to the east of that island the boat went to, from whence also a shoal-point stretched out itself till it met the other: they brought with them such a cockle as I have mentioned in my "Voyage Round the World" found near Celebes, and they saw many more, some bigger than that which they brought aboard, as they said, and for this reason I named it Cockle Island. I sent them to sound again, ordering them to fire a musket if they found good anchoring; we were then standing to the southward, with a fine breeze. As soon as they fired, I tacked and stood in; they told me they had fifty fathom when they fired. I tacked again, and made all the sail I could to get out, being near some rocky islands and shoals to leeward of us. The breeze increased, and I thought we were out of danger, but having a shoal just by us, and the wind falling again, I ordered the boat to tow us, and by their help we got clear from it. We had a strong tide setting to the westward.

At one o'clock, being past the shoal, and finding the tide setting to the westward, I anchored in thirty-five fathom coarse sand, with small coral and shells. Being nearest to Cockle Island, I immediately sent both the

boats thither, one to cut wood, and the other to fish.
At four in the afternoon, having a small breeze at
south-south-west, I made a sign for my boats to come
on board. They brought some wood, and a few small
cockles, none of them exceeding ten pounds' weight,
whereas the shell of the great one weighed seventy-
eight pounds; but it was now high water, and therefore
they could get no bigger. They also brought on board
some pigeons, of which we found plenty on all the
islands where we touched in these seas: also in many
places we saw many large bats, but killed none, except
those I mentioned at Pulo Sabuda. As our boats came
aboard, we weighed and made sail, steering east-south-
east as long as the wind held. In the morning we
found we had got four or five leagues to the east of the
place where we weighed. We stood to and fro till
eleven; and finding that we lost ground, anchored in
forty-two fathom coarse gravelly sand, with some coral.
This morning we thought we saw a sail.

In the afternoon I went ashore on a small woody
island. about two leagues from us. Here I found the
greatest number of pigeons that ever I saw either in
the East or West Indies, and small cockles in the sea
round the island in such quantities that we might have
laden the boat in an hour's time. These were not
above ten or twelve pounds' weight. We cut some
wood, and brought off cockles enough for all the ship's
company; but having no small shot, we could kill no
pigeons. I returned about four o'clock, and then my

gunner and both mates went thither, and in less than three-quarters of an hour they killed and brought off ten pigeons. Here is a tide: the flood sets west and the ebb east, but the latter is very faint and but of small continuance, and so we found it ever since we came from Timor: the winds we found easterly, between north-east and east-south-east, so that if these continue, it is impossible to beat farther to the eastward on this coast against wind and current. These easterly winds increased from the time we were in the latitude of about 2° south, and as we drew nigher the line they hung more easterly: and now being to the north of the continent of New Guinea, where the coast lies east and west, I find the trade-wind here at east, which yet in higher latitudes is usually at north-north-west and north-west; and so I did expect them here, it being to the south of the line.

The 7th, in the morning, I sent my boat ashore on Pigeon Island, and stayed till noon. In the afternoon my men returned, brought twenty-two pigeons, and many cockles, some very large, some small: they also brought one empty shell, that weighed two hundred and fifty-eight pounds.

At four o'clock we weighed, having a small westerly wind and a tide with us; at seven in the evening we anchored in forty-two fathom, near King William's Island, where I went ashore the next morning, drank His Majesty's health, and honoured it with his name. It is about two leagues and a half in length, very high and extraordinarily well clothed with woods; the trees are of divers sorts, most unknown to us, but all very green and flourishing; many of them had flowers, some white, some purple, others yellow : all which smelt very fragrantly : the trees are generally tall and straight bodied, and may be fit for any use. I saw one of a clean body, without knot or limb, sixty or seventy feet high by estimation; it was three of my fathoms about, and kept its bigness, without any sensible decrease, even to the top. The mould of the island is black, but not deep, it being very rocky. On the sides and top of the island are many palmetto trees, whose heads we could discern over all the other trees, but their bodies we could not see.

About one in the afternoon we weighed and stood to the eastward, between the main and King William's Island, leaving the island on our larboard side, and sounding till we were past the island, and then we had no ground. Here we found the flood setting east-by-north, and the ebb west-by-south ; there were shoals and small islands between us and the main, which caused the tide to set very inconstantly, and make many whirlings in the water; yet we did not find the tide to set strong any way, nor the water to rise much.

On the 9th, being to the eastward of King William's Island, we plied all day between the main and other islands, having easterly winds and fair weather till seven the next morning ; then we had very hard rain till eight, and saw many shoals of fish. We lay becalmed off a pretty deep bay on New Guinea, about twelve or fourteen leagues wide, and seven or eight leagues deep, having low land near its bottom, but high land without.   The easternmost part of New Guinea seen bore east-by-south, distant twelve leagues ; Capo Mabo west-south-west half-south, distant seven leagues.

At one in the afternoon it began to rain, and continued till six in the evening, so that, having but little wind and most calms, we lay still off the forementioned bay, having King William's Island still in sight, though distant by judgment fifteen or sixteen leagues west.   We saw many shoals of small fish, some sharks, and seven or eight dolphins, but caught none.   In the afternoon, being about four leagues from the shore, we saw an opening in the land, which seemed to afford good harbour.   In the evening we saw a large fire there, and I intended to go in (if winds and weather would permit) to get some acquaintance with the natives.

Since the 4th instant that we passed Capo Mabo, to the 12th, we had small easterly winds and calms, so that we anchored several times, where I made my men cut wood, that we might have a good stock when a westerly wind should present, and so we plied to the eastward, as winds and currents would permit, having not got in all above thirty leagues to the eastward of Cape Mabo ; but on the 12th, at four in the afternoon, a small gale sprang up at north-east-by-north, with rain ; at five it shuffled about to north-west, from

thence to the south-west, and continued between those
two points a pretty brisk gale, so that we made sail
and steered away north-east, till the 13th, in the
morning, to get about the Cape of Good Hope. When
it was day we steered north-east half east, then north-
east-by-east till seven o'clock, and, being then seven or
eight leagues off shore, we steered away east, the shore
trending east-by-south. We had very much rain all
night, so that we could not carry much sail, yet we had
a very steady gale. At eight this morning the weather
cleared up, and the wind decreased to a fine top-gallant
gale, and settled at west-by-south. We had more rain
these three days past, than all the voyage, in so short a
time. We were now about six leagues from the land
of New Guinea, which appeared very high; and we
saw two headlands about twenty leagues asunder, the
one to the east and the other to the west, which last
is called the Cape of Good Hope. We found variation
east 4°.

The 15th, in the morning, between twelve and two
o'clock, it blew a very brisk gale at north-west, and
looked very black in the south-west. At two it flew
about at once to the south-south-west, and rained very
hard. The wind settled some time at west-south-west,
and we steered east-north-east till three in the morning;
then the wind and rain abating, we steered east-half-
north for fear of coming near the land. Presently
after, it being a little clear, the man at the bowsprit end
called out, "Land on our starboard bow." We looked out

and saw it plain : I presently sounded, and had but ten fathom, soft ground. The master, being somewhat scared, came running in haste with this news, and said it was best to anchor. I told him no, but sound again; then we had twelve fathom; the next cast, thirteen and a half; the fourth, seventeen fathom; and then no ground with fifty fathom line. However, we kept off the island, and did not go so fast but that we could see any other danger before we came nigh it; for here might have been more islands not laid down in my drafts besides this, for I searched all the drafts I had, if perchance I might find any island in the one which was not in the others, but I could find none near us. When it was day we were about five leagues off the land we saw; but, I believe, not above five miles, or at most two leagues, off it when we first saw it in the night.

This is a small island, but 'pretty high ; I named it Providence. About five leagues to the southward of this there is another island, which is called William Scouten's Island, and laid down in our drafts: it is a high island, and about twenty leagues long.

It was by mere providence that we missed the small island ; for, had not the wind come to west-south-west, and blown hard, so that we steered east-north-east, we had been upon it by our course that we steered before, if we could not have seen it. This morning we saw many great trees and logs swim by us, which, it is probable, came out of some great rivers on the main.

On the 16th we crossed the line, and found variation 6° 26' east.   The 18th, by my observation at noon, we found that we had had a current setting to the southward, and probably that drew us in so nigh Scouten's Island.   For this twenty-four hours we steered east-by-north with a large wind, yet made but an east-by-south half south course, though the variation was not above 7° east.

The 21st we had a current setting to the northward, which is against the true trade monsoon, it being now near the full moon.   I did expect it here, as in all other places.   We had variation 8° 45' east.   The 22nd we found but little current, if any; it set to the southward.

On the 23rd, in the afternoon, we saw two snakes, and the next morning another passing by us, which was furiously assaulted by two fishes, that had kept us company five or six days; they were shaped like mackerel, and were about that bigness and length, and of a yellow-greenish colour.   The snake swam away from them very fast, keeping his head above water; the fish snapped at his tail, but when he turned himself, that fish would withdraw, and another would snap, so that by turns they kept him employed, yet he still defended himself, and swam away a great pace, till they were out of sight.

The 25th, betimes in the morning, we saw an island to the southward of us, at about fifteen leagues' distance. We steered away for it, supposing it to be that which the Dutch call Wishart's Island; but, finding it otherwise, I called it Matthias, it being that saint's day. This island is about nine or ten leagues long, mountainous and woody, with many savannahs, and some spots of land which seemed to be cleared.

At eight in the evening we lay by, intending, if I could, to anchor under Matthias Isle; but the next morning, seeing another island about seven or eight leagues to the eastward of it, we steered away for it. At noon we came up fair with its south-west end, intending to run along by it and anchor on the south-east side, but the tornadoes came in so thick and hard that I could not venture in. This island is pretty low and plain, and clothed with wood; the trees were very green, and appeared to be large and tall, as thick as they could stand one by another. It is about two or three leagues long, and at the south-west point there is another small, low, woody island, about a mile round, and about a mile from the other. Between them there runs a reef of rocks which joins them. (The biggest I named Squally Island.)

Seeing we could not anchor here, I stood away to the southward, to make the main; but having many hard squalls and tornadoes, we were often forced to hand all our sails and steer more easterly to go before it. On the 26th at four o'clock it cleared up to a hard sky and a brisk settled gale; then we made as much sail as we could. At five it cleared up over the land, and we saw, as we thought, Cape Solomaswer bearing south-south-east, distance ten leagues. We had many great logs and trees swimming by us all this afternoon, and much grass; we steered in south-south-east till six, then the wind slackened, and we stood off till seven, having little wind; then we lay by till ten, at which time we made sail, and steered away east all night. The next morning, as soon as it was light, we made all the sail we could, and steered away east-south-east, as the land lay, being fair in sight of it, and not above seven leagues' distance. We passed by many small low woody islands which lay between us and the main, not laid down in our drafts. We found variation 9° 50′ east.

The 28th we had many violent tornadoes, wind, rain, and some spouts, and in the tornadoes the wind shifted. In the night we ¦had ¦fair weather, but more lightning than we had seen at any time this voyage. This morning we left a large high island on our larboard side, called in the Dutch drafts Wishart's Isle, about six leagues from the main; and, seeing many smokes upon the main, I therefore steered towards it.

The mainland at this place is high and mountainous, adorned with tall, flourishing trees; the sides of the hills had many large plantations and patches of clear land, which, together with the smoke we saw, were certain signs of its being well inhabited; and I was desirous to have some commerce with the inhabitants. Being nigh shore, we saw first one proa; a little after. two or three more, and at last a great many boats came from all the adjacent bays. When they were forty-six in number they approached so near us that we could see each other's signs and hear each other speak, though we could not understand them, nor they us. They made signs for us to go in towards the shore, pointing that way. It was squally weather, which at first made me cautious of going too near; but the weather beginning to look pretty well, I endeavoured to get into a bay ahead of us, which we could have got into well enough at first; but while we lay by, we were driven so far to leeward that now it was more difficult to get in. The natives lay in their proas round us; to whom I showed beads, knives, glasses, to allure them to come nearer. But they would not come so nigh as to receive anything from us; therefore I threw out some things to them, viz., a knife fastened to a piece of board, and a glass bottle corked up with some beads in it, which they took up, and seemed well pleased. They often struck their left breast with their right hand, and as often held up a black truncheon over their heads, which we thought was a token of friendship, wherefore we did the like. And when we stood in towards their shore, they seemed to rejoice; but when we stood off, they frowned, yet kept us company in their proas, still pointing to the shore. About five o'clock we got within the mouth of the bay, and sounded several times, but had no ground, though within a mile of the shore. The basin of this bay was about two miles within us, into which we might have gone; but as I was not

assured of anchorage there, so I thought it not prudent
to run in at this time, it being near night, and seeing a
black tornado rising in the west, which I most feared.
Besides, we had near two hundred men in proas close
by us; and the bays on the shore were lined with men
from one end to the other, where there could not be
less than three or four hundred more. What weapons
they had, we knew not, nor yet their design ; therefore
I had, at their first coming near us, got up all our
small arms, and made several put on cartouch boxes, to
prevent treachery. At last I resolved to go out again ;
which, when the natives in their proas perceived, they
began to fling stones at us as fast as they could, being
provided with engines for that purpose, wherefore I
named this place Slinger's Bay ; but at the firing of
one gun they were all amazed, drew off, and flung
no more stones. They got together, as if consulting
what to do ; for they did not make in towards the
shore, but lay still, though some of them were killed
or wounded ; and many more of them had paid for
their boldness, but that I was unwilling to cut off any
of them, which, if I had done, I could not hope afterwards to bring them to treat with me.

The next day we sailed close by an island, where we
saw many smokes, and men in the bays, out of which
came two or three canoes, taking much pains to over-
take us, but they could not, though we went with an
easy sail, and I could not now stay for them. As I
passed by the south-east point I sounded several times

within a mile of the Sandy Bays, but had no ground. About three leagues to the northward of the south-east point we opened a large, deep bay, secured from west-north-west and south-west winds. There were two other islands that lay to the north-east of it, which secured the bay from north-east winds; one was but small, yet woody; the other was a league long, inhabited, and full of cocoa-nut trees. I endeavoured to get into this bay, but there came such flaws off from the high land over it that I could not. Besides, we had many hard squalls, which deterred me from it; and, night coming on, I would not run any hazard, but bore away to the small inhabited island, to see if we could get anchorage on the east side of it. When we came there we found the island so narrow, that there could be no shelter; therefore I tacked and stood towards the greater island again; and being more than midway between both, I lay by, designing to endeavour for anchorage next morning. Between seven and eight at night we spied a canoe close by us, and seeing no more, suffered her to come aboard. She had three men in her, who brought off five cocoa-nuts, for which I gave each of them a knife and a string of beads, to encourage them to come off again in the morning: but before these went away we saw two more canoes coming; therefore we stood away to the northward from them, and then lay by again till day. We saw no more boats this night, neither designed to suffer any to come aboard in the dark.

P 13

By nine o'clock the next morning we were got within a league of the great island, but were kept off by violent gusts of wind. These squalls gave us warning of their approach by the clouds which hung over the mountains, and afterwards descended to the foot of them; and then it is we expect them speedily.

On the 3rd of March, being about five leagues to leeward of the great island, we saw the mainland ahead, and another great high island to leeward of us, distant about seven leagues, which we bore away for. It is called in the Dutch drafts Garret Dennis Isle. It is about fourteen or fifteen leagues round, high and mountainous, and very woody. Some trees appeared very large and tall, and the bays by the seaside are well stored with cocoa-nut trees, where we also saw some small houses. The sides of the mountains are thick-set with plantations, and the mould in the new-cleared land seemed to be of a brown-reddish colour. This island is of no regular figure, but is full of points shooting forth into the sea, between which are many sandy bays, full of cocoa-nut trees. The middle of the isle lies in 3° 10′ south latitude. It is very populous. The natives are very black, strong, and well-limbed people, having great round heads, their hair naturally curled and short, which they shave into several forms, and dye it also of divers colours—viz., red, white, and yellow. They have broad round faces, with great bottle-noses, yet agreeable enough till they disfigure them by painting, and by wearing great things through their noses as big as a man's thumb, and about four inches long. These are run clear through both nostrils, one end coming out by one cheek-bone, and the other end against the other; and their noses so stretched that only a small slip of them appears about the ornament. They have also great holes in their ears, wherein they wear such stuff as in their noses. They are very dexterous, active fellows in their proas, which are very ingeniously built. They are narrow and long, with outriggers on one side, the head and stern higher than the rest, and carved into many devices— viz., some fowl, fish, or a man's head painted or carved; and though it is but rudely done, yet the resemblance appears plainly, and shows an ingenious fancy. But with what instruments they make their proas or carved work I know not, for they seem to be utterly ignorant of iron. They have very neat paddles, with which they manage their proas dexterously, and make great way through the water. Their weapons are chiefly lances. swords and slings, and some bows and arrows. They have also wooden fish-spears for striking fish. Those that came to assault us in Slinger's Bay on the main are in all respects like these, and I believe these are alike treacherous. Their speech is clear and distinct. The words they used most when near us were *racousce allamais*, and then they pointed to the shore. Their signs of friendship are either a great truncheon, or bough of a tree full of leaves, put on their heads, often striking their heads with their hands.

The next day, having a fresh gale of wind, we got under a high island, about four or five leagues round, very woody, and full of plantations upon the sides of the hills; and in the bays, by the waterside, are abundance of cocoa-nut trees. It lies in the latitude of 3° 25′ south, and meridian distance from Cape Mabo 1,316 miles. On the south-east part of it are three or four other small woody islands, one high and peaked, the others low and flat, all bedecked with cocoa-nut trees and other wood. On the north there is another island of an indifferent height and of a somewhat larger circumference than the great high island last mentioned. We passed between this and the high island. The high island is called in the Dutch drafts Anthony Cave's Island. As for the flat, low island, and the other small one, it is probable they were never seen by the Dutch, nor the islands to the north of Garret Dennis's Island. As soon as we came near Cave's Island some canoes came about us, and made signs for us to come ashore, as all the rest had done before, probably thinking we could run the ship aground anywhere, as they did their proas, for we saw neither sail nor anchor among any of them, though most Eastern Indians have both. These had proas made of one tree, well dug, with outriggers on one side; they were but small, yet well shaped. We endeavoured to anchor, but found no ground within a mile of the shore. We kept close along the north side, still sounding till we came to the north-east end, but found no ground, the canoes still accompanying us, and the bays were covered with men going along as we sailed. Many of them strove to swim off to us, but we left them astern. Being at the north-east point, we found a strong current setting to the north-west, so that though we had steered to keep under the high island, yet we were driven towards the flat one. At this time three of the natives came on board. I gave each of them a knife, a looking-glass, and a string of beads. I showed them pumpkins and cocoa-nut shells, and made signs to them to bring some aboard, and had presently three cocoa-nuts out of one of the canoes. I showed them nutmegs, and by their signs I guessed they had some on the island. I also showed them some gold dust, which they seemed to know, and called out "Manneel, Manneel," and pointed towards the land. A while after these men were gone, two or three canoes came from the flat island, and by signs invited us to their island, at which the others seemed displeased, and used very menacing gestures and, I believe, speeches to each other. Night coming on, we stood off to sea, and having but little wind all night, were driven away to the north-west. We saw many great fires on the flat island. The last men that came off to us were all black as those we had seen before, with frizzled hair. They were very tall, lusty, well-shaped men. They wear great things in their noses, and paint as the others, but not much. They make the same signs of friendship, and their language seems to be one; but the others had proas, and these canoes. On the sides of some of these we saw the figures of several fish neatly cut, and these last were not so shy as the others.

Steering away from Cave's Island south-south-east, we found a strong current against us, which set only in some places in streams, and in them we saw many trees and logs of wood, which drove by us. We had but little wood aboard; wherefore I hoisted out the pinnace, and sent her to take up some of this drift-wood. In a little time she came aboard with a great tree in tow, which we could hardly hoist in with all our tackles. We cut up the tree and split it for firewood. It was much worm-eaten, and had in it some live worms above an inch long, and about the bigness of a goose-quill, and having their heads crusted over with a thin shell.

After this we passed by an island, called by the Dutch St. John's Island, leaving it to the north of us. It is about nine or ten leagues round, and very well adorned with lofty trees. We saw many plantations on the sides of the hills, and abundance of cocoa-nut trees about them, as also thick groves on the bays by the seaside. As we came near it three canoes came off to us, but would not come aboard. They were such as we had seen about the other islands. They spoke the same language, and made the same signs of peace, and their canoes were such as at Cave's Island.

We stood along by St. John's Island till we came almost to the south-east point, and then, seeing no more islands to the eastward of us, nor any likelihood

of anchoring under this, I steered away for the main of
New Guinea, we being now, as I supposed, to the east
of it, on this north side. My design of seeing these
islands as I passed along was to get wood and water,
but could find no anchor ground, and therefore could
not do as I purposed; besides, these islands are all so
populous, that I dared not send my boat ashore, unless
I could have anchored pretty nigh; wherefore I rather
chose to prosecute my design on the main, the season
of the year being now at hand, for I judged the westerly
winds were nigh spent.

On the 8th of March we saw some smoke on the
main, being distant from it four or five leagues. It is
very high, woody land, with some spots of savannah.
About ten in the morning six or seven canoes came off
to us. Most of them had no more than one man in
them. They were all black, with short curled hair,
having the same ornaments in their noses, and their
heads so shaved and painted, and speaking the same
words as the inhabitants of Cave's Island before
mentioned.

There was a headland to the southward of us,
beyond which, seeing no land, I supposed that from
thence the land trends away more westerly. This
headland lies in the latitude of 5° 2' south, and
meridian distance from Cape Mabo 1,290 miles. In
the night we lay by, for fear of overshooting this
headland, between which and Cape St. Maries the
land is high, mountainous and woody, having many

points of land shooting out into the sea, which make so many fine bays; the coast lies north-north-east and south-south-west.

The 9th, in the morning a huge black man came off to us in a canoe, but would not come aboard. He made the same signs of friendship to us as the rest we had met with; yet seemed to differ in his language, not using any of those words which the others did. We saw neither smoke nor plantations near this head-land. We found here variation 1° east.

In the afternoon, as we plied near the shore, three canoes came off to us; one had four men in her, the others two apiece. That with the four men came pretty nigh us, and showed us a cocoa-nut and water in a bamboo, making signs that there was enough ashore where they lived; they pointed to the place where they would have us go, and so went away. We saw a small round pretty high island about a league to the north of this headland, within which there was a large deep bay, whither the canoes went; and we strove to get thither before night, but could not; wherefore we stood off, and saw land to the westward of this headland, bearing west-by-south-half-south, distance about ten leagues, and, as we thought, still more land bearing south-west-by-south, distance twelve or fourteen leagues, but being clouded, it disappeared, and we thought we had been deceived. Before night we opened the headland fair, and I named it Cape St. George. The land from hence trends away west-north-west about ten leagues, which is as far as we could see it ; and the land that we saw to the westward of it in the evening, which bore west-by-south-half-south, was another point about ten leagues from Cape St. George ; between which there runs in a deep bay for twenty leagues or more. We saw some high land in spots like islands, down in that bay at a great distance; but whether they are islands, or the main closing there we know not. The next morning we saw other land to the south-east of the westernmost point, which till then was clouded; it was very high land, and the same that we saw the day before, that disappeared in a cloud. This Cape St. George lies in the latitude of 5° 5′ south; and meridian distance from Cape Mabo 1,290 miles. The island off this cape I called St. George's Isle; and the bay between it and the west point I named St. George's Bay. [Note :—No Dutch drafts go so far as this cape by ten leagues.] On the 10th, in the evening, we got within a league of the westernmost land seen, which is pretty high and very woody, but no appearance of anchoring. I stood off again, designing, if possible, to ply to and fro in this bay till I found a conveniency to wood and water. We saw no more plantations nor cocoa-nut trees; yet in the night we discerned a small fire right against us. The next morning we saw a burning mountain in the country. It was round, high, and peaked at top, as most volcanoes are, and sent forth a great quantity of smoke. We took up a log of driftwood, and split it for firing; in which we found some small fish.

The day after we passed by the south-west cape of this bay, leaving it to the north of us. When we were abreast of it I called my officers together, and named it Cape Orford, in honour of my noble patron, drinking his Lordship's health. This cape bears from Cape St. George south-west about eighteen leagues. Between them there is a bay about twenty-five leagues deep, having pretty high land all round it, especially near the capes. though they themselves are not high. Cape Orford lies in the latitude of 5° 24′ south, by my observation; and meridian distance from Cape St. George, forty-four miles west. The land trends from this cape north-west by west into the bay, and on the other side south-west per compass, which is south-west 9° west, allowing the variation, which is here 9° east. The land on each side of the cape is more savannah than woodland, and is highest on the north-west side. The cape itself is a bluff-point, of an indifferent height, with a flat tableland at top. When we were to the south-west of the cape, it appeared to be a low point shooting out, which you cannot see when abreast of it. This morning we struck a log of driftwood with our turtle-irons, hoisted it in, and split it for firewood. Afterwards we struck another, but could not get it in. There were many fish about it.

We steered along south-west as the land lies, keeping about six leagues off the shore; and, being desirous to cut wood and fill water, if I saw any conveniency, I lay by in the night, because I would not miss any place proper for those ends, for fear of wanting such necessaries as we could not live without. This coast is high and mountainous, and not so thick with trees as that on the other side of Cape Orford.

On the 14th, seeing a pretty deep bay ahead, and some islands where I thought we might ride secure, we ran in towards the shore and saw some smoke. At ten o'clock we saw a point which shot out pretty well into the sea, with a bay within it, which promised fair for water; and we stood in with a moderate gale. Being got into the bay within the point, we saw many cocoa-nut-trees, plantations, and houses. When I came within four or five miles of the shore, six small boats came off to view us, with about forty men in them all. Perceiving that they only came to view us, and would not come aboard, I made signs and waved to them to go ashore; but they did not or would not understand me; therefore I whistled a shot over their heads out of my fowling-piece, and then they pulled away for the shore as hard as they could. These were no sooner ashore, than we saw three boats coming from the islands to leeward of us, and they soon came within call, for we lay becalmed. One of the boats had about forty men in her, and was a large, well-built boat; the other two were but small. Not long after, I saw another boat coming out of the bay where I intended to go; she likewise was a large boat,

with a high head and stern painted, and full of men.
This I thought came off to fight us, as it is probable
they all did; therefore I fired another small shot over
the great boat that was nigh us, which made them
leave their babbling and take to their paddles. We
still lay becalmed; and therefore they, rowing wide of
us, directed their course towards the other great boat
that was coming off. When they were pretty near each
other I caused the gunner to fire a gun between them,
which he did very dexterously; it was loaded with
round and partridge shot; the last dropped in the
water somewhat short of them, but the round shot
went between both boats, and grazed about one
hundred yards beyond them. This so affrighted them
that they both rowed away for the shore as fast as
they could, without coming near each other; and the
little boats made the best of their way after them.
And now, having a gentle breeze at south-south-east,
we bore into the bay after them. When we came by
the point, I saw a great number of men peeping from
under the rocks: I ordered a shot to be fired close by,
to scare them. The shot grazed between us and the
point, and, mounting again, flew over the point, and
grazed a second time just by them. We were obliged
to sail along close by the bays; and, seeing multitudes
sitting under the trees, I ordered a third gun to be fired
among the cocoa-nut-trees to scare them; for my business
being to wood and water, I thought it necessary to strike
some terror into the inhabitants, who were very numerous,

and (by what I saw now, and had formerly experienced) treacherous. After this I sent my boat to sound; they had first forty, then thirty, and at last twenty fathom water. We followed the boat, and came to anchor about a quarter of a mile from the shore, in twenty-six fathom water, fine black sand and ooze. We rode right against the mouth of a small river, where I hoped to find fresh water. Some of the natives standing on a small point at the river's mouth, I sent a small shot over their heads to frighten them, which it did effectually. In the afternoon I sent my boat ashore to the natives who stood upon the point by the river's mouth with a present of cocoa-nuts; when the boat was come near the shore, they came running into the water, and put their nuts into the boat. Then I made a signal for the boat to come aboard, and sent both it and the yawl into the river to look for fresh water, ordering the pinnace to lie near the river's mouth, while the yawl went up to search. In an hour's time they returned aboard with some barrecoes full fresh of water, which they had taken up about half a mile up the river. After which I sent them again with casks, ordering one of them to fill water, and the other to watch the motions of the natives, lest they should make any opposition. But they did not, and so the boats returned a little before sunset with a tun and a half of water; and the next day by noon brought aboard about six tuns of water.

I sent ashore commodities to purchase hogs, &c.

being informed that the natives have plenty of them, as also of yams and other good roots; but my men returned without getting anything that I sent them for, the natives being unwilling to trade with us. Yet they admired our hatchets and axes, but would part with nothing but cocoa-nuts, which they used to climb the trees for; and so soon as they gave them our men, they beckoned to them to be gone, for they were much afraid of us.

The 18th I sent both boats again for water, and before noon they had filled all my casks. In the afternoon I sent them both to cut wood; but seeing about forty natives standing on the bay at a small distance from our men, I made a signal for them to come aboard again, which they did, and brought me word that the men which we saw on the bay were passing that way, but were afraid to come nigh them. At four o'clock I sent both the boats again for more wood, and they returned in the evening. Then I called my officers to consult whether it were convenient to stay here longer, and endeavour a better acquaintance with these people, or go to sea. My design of tarrying here longer was, if possible, to get some hogs, goats, yams, or other roots, as also to get some knowledge of the country and its product. My officers unanimously gave their opinions for staying longer here. So the next day I sent both boats ashore again, to fish and to cut more wood. While they were ashore about thirty or forty men and women passed by them; they were a

little afraid of our people at first, but upon their
making signs of friendship, they passed by quietly, the
men finely bedecked with feathers of divers colours
about their heads, and lances in their hands ; the
women had no ornament about them, nor anything to
cover their nakedness but a bunch of small green
boughs before and behind, stuck under a string which
came round their waists. They carried large baskets
on their heads, full of yams. And this I have observed
amongst all the wild natives I have known, that they
make their women carry the burdens while the men
walk before, without any other load than their arms
and ornaments. At noon our men came aboard with
the wood they had cut, and had caught but six fishes
at four or five hauls of the seine, though we saw
abundance of fish leaping in the bay all the day long.

In the afternoon I sent the boats ashore for more
wood ; and some of our men went to the natives'
houses, and found they were now more shy than they
used to be, had taken down all the cocoa-nuts from
the trees, and driven away their hogs. Our people
made signs to them to know what was become of their
hogs, &c. The natives pointing to some houses in the
bottom of the bay, and imitating the noise of those
creatures, seemed to intimate that there were both hogs
and goats of several sizes, which they expressed by
holding their hands abroad at several distances from
the ground.

At night our boats came aboard with wood, and the

next morning I went myself with both boats up the river to the watering-place, carrying with me all such trifles and iron-work as I thought most proper to induce them to a commerce with us; but I found them very shy and roguish. I saw but two men and a boy. One of the men, by some signs, was persuaded to come to the boat's side, where I was; to him I gave a knife, a string of beads, and a glass bottle. The fellow called out, "Cocos, cocos," pointing to a village hard by, and signified to us that he would go for some; but he never returned to us: and thus they had frequently of late served our men. I took eight or nine men with me, and marched to their houses, which I found very mean, and their doors made fast with withies.

I visited three of their villages, and, finding all the houses thus abandoned by the inhabitants, who carried with them all their hogs, &c., I brought out of their houses some small fishing-nets in recompense for those things they had received of us. As we were coming away we saw two of the natives; I showed them the things that we carried with us, and called to them, "Cocos, cocos," to let them know that I took these things because they had not made good what they had promised by their signs, and by their calling out "Cocos." While I was thus employed the men in the yawl filled two hogsheads of water, and all the barrecoes. About one in the afternoon I came aboard, and found all my officers and men very importunate to go to that bay where the hogs were said to be. I was

loth to yield to it, fearing they would deal too roughly
with the natives. By two o'clock in the afternoon
many black clouds gathered over the land, which I
thought would deter them from their enterprise; but
they solicited me the more to let them go. At last I
consented, sending those commodities I had ashore
with me in the morning, and giving them a strict
charge to deal by fair means, and to act cautiously for
their own security. The bay I sent them to was about
two miles from the ship. As soon as they were gone,
I got all things ready, that, if I saw occasion, I might
assist them with my great guns. When they came to
land, the natives in great companies stood to resist
them, shaking their lances, and threatening them, and
some were so daring as to wade into the sea, holding a
target in one hand and a lance in the other. Our men
held up to them such commodities as I had sent, and
made signs of friendship, but to no purpose, for the
natives waved them off. Seeing, therefore, they could
not be prevailed upon to a friendly commerce, my
men, being resolved to have some provision among
them, fired some muskets to scare them away, which
had the desired effect upon all but two or three, who
stood still in a menacing posture, till the boldest
dropped his target and ran away. They supposed he
was shot in the arm; he and some others felt the
smart of our bullets, but none were killed, our design
being rather to frighten than to kill them. Our men
landed, and found abundance of tame hogs running

among the houses. They shot down nine, which they brought away, besides many that ran away wounded. They had but little time, for in less than an hour after they went from the ship it began to rain; wherefore they got what they could into the boats, for I had charged them to come away if it rained. By the time the boat was aboard and the hogs taken in it cleared up, and my men desired to make another trip thither before night; this was about five in the evening, and I consented, giving them orders to repair on board before night. In the close of the evening they returned accordingly, with eight hogs more, and a little live pig; and by this time the other hogs were jerked and salted. These that came last we only dressed and corned till morning, and then sent both boats ashore for more refreshments either of hogs or roots; but in the night the natives had conveyed away their provisions of all sorts. Many of them were now about the houses, and none offered to resist our boats landing, but, on the contrary, were so amicable, that one man brought ten or twelve cocoa-nuts, left them on the shore after he had shown them to our men, and went out of sight. Our people, finding nothing but nets and images, brought some of them|away, which two of my men brought aboard in a small canoe, and presently after my boats came off. I ordered the boatswain to take care of the nets till we came at some place where they might be disposed of for some re-freshment for the use of all the company. The images I took into my own custody.

In the afternoon I sent the canoe to the place from whence she had been brought, and in her two axes, two hatchets (one of them helved), six knives, six looking-glasses, a large bunch of beads, and four glass bottles. Our men drew the canoe ashore, placed the things to the best advantage in her, and came off in the pinnace which I sent to guard them; and now, being well-stocked with wood and all my water-casks full, I resolved to sail the next morning. All the time of our stay here we had very fair weather, only sometimes in the afternoon we had a shower of rain, which lasted not above an hour at most; also some thunder and lightning, with very little wind; we had sea and land breezes, the former between the south-south-east, and the latter from north-east to north-west.

This place I named Port Montague in honour of my noble patron: it lies in the latitude of 6° 10′ south, and meridian distance from Cape St. George 151 miles west. The country hereabouts is mountainous and woody, full of rich valleys and pleasant fresh-water brooks. The mould in the valleys is deep and yellowish, that on the sides of the hill of a very brown colour, and not very deep, but rocky underneath, yet excellent planting land. The trees in general are neither very straight, thick, nor tall, yet appear green and pleasant enough; some of them bore flowers, some berries, and others big fruits, but all unknown to any of us; cocoa-nut trees thrive very well

here, as well on the bays by the sea-side, as more
remote among the plantations; the nuts are of an
indifferent size, the milk and kernel very thick and
pleasant.   Here is ginger, yams, and other very good
roots for the pot, that our men saw and tasted; what
other fruits or roots the country affords I know not.
Here are hogs and dogs; other land-animals we saw
none.   The fowls we saw and knew were pigeons,
parrots, cockatoos, and crows like those in England;
a sort of birds about the bigness of a blackbird, and
smaller birds many.   The sea and rivers have plenty
of fish; we saw abundance, though we caught but few,
and these were cavallies, yellow-tails, and whip-rays.

We departed from hence on the 22nd of March, and
on the 24th, in the evening, we saw some high land
bearing north-west half-west, to the west of which we
could see no land, though there appeared something
like land bearing west a little southerly, but not being
sure of it, I steered west-north-west all night, and kept
going on with an easy sail, intending to coast along the
shore at a distance.   At ten o'clock I saw a great fire
bearing north-west-by-west, blazing up in a pillar,
sometimes very high for three or four minutes, then
falling quite down for an equal space of time, sometimes
hardly visible, till it blazed up again.   I had laid me
down, having been indisposed these three days; but
upon a sight of this, my chief mate called me; I got
up and viewed it for about half an hour, and knew it to
be a burning hill by its intervals: I charged them to

look well out, having bright moonlight. In the morning I found that the fire we had seen the night before was a burning island, and steered for it. We saw many other islands, one large high island, and another smaller but pretty high. I stood near the volcano, and many small low islands, with some shoals.

March the 25th, 1700, in the evening we came within three leagues of this burning hill, being at the same time two leagues from the main; I found a good channel to pass between them, and kept nearer the main than the island. At seven in the evening I sounded, and had fifty-two fathom fine sand and ooze. I stood to the northward to get clear of this strait, having but little wind and fair weather. The island all night vomited fire and smoke very amazingly, and at every belch we heard a dreadful noise like thunder, and saw a flame of fire after it the most terrifying that ever I saw; the intervals between its belches were about half a minute, some more, others less; neither were these pulses or eruptions alike, for some were but faint convulsions, in comparison of the more vigorous; yet even the weakest vented a great deal of fire; but the largest made a roaring noise, and sent up a large flame, twenty or thirty yards high; and then might be seen a great stream of fire running down to the foot of the island, even to the shore. From the furrows made by this descending fire, we could, in the day time, see great smoke arise, which probably were made by the sulphurous matter thrown out of the funnel at the top,

which tumbling down to the bottom, and there lying
in a heap, burned till either consumed or extinguished;
and as long as it burned and kept its heat, so long the
smoke ascended from it; which we perceived to increase
or decrease, according to the quantity of matter discharged from the funnel: but the next night, being
shot to the westward of the burning island, and the
funnel of it lying on the south side, we could not
discern the fire there, as we did the smoke in the
the day when we were to the southward of it. This
volcano lies in the latitude of 5° 33′ south, and meridian
distance from Cape St. George, three hundred and
thirty-two miles west.

The easternmost part of New Guinea lies forty miles
to the westward of this tract of land; and by hydro-
graphers they are made joining together; but here I
found an opening and passage between, with many
islands, the largest of which lie on the north side of
this passage or strait. The channel is very good, between the islands and the land to the eastward. The east
part of New Guinea is high and mountainous, ending
on the north-east with a large promontory, which I
named King William's Cape, in honour of his present
Majesty. We saw some smoke on it, and leaving it on
our larboard side, steered away near the east land, which
ends with two remarkable capes or heads, distant from
each other about six or seven leagues: within each head
were two very remarkable mountains, ascending very
gradually from the sea-side, which afforded a very

pleasant and agreeable prospect. The mountains and
the lower land were pleasantly mixed with woodland
and savannahs; the trees appeared very green and
flourishing, and the savannahs seemed to be very
smooth and even; no meadow in England appears more
green in the spring than these. We saw smoke, but
did not strive to anchor here, but rather chose to get
under one of the islands (where I thought I should
find few or no inhabitants), that I might repair my
pinnace, which was so crazy that I could not venture
ashore anywhere with her. As we stood over to the
islands, we looked out very well to the north, but could
see no land that way; by which I was well assured
that we were got through, and that this east land does
not join to New Guinea; therefore I named it Nova
Britannia. The north-west cape I called Cape Gloucester, and the south-west-point Cape Anne; and the
north-west mountain, which is very remarkable, I called
Mount Gloucester.

This island which I called Nova Britannia, has
about 4° of latitude: the body of it lying in 4°, and
the northernmost part in 2° 32′, and the southernmost
in 6° 30′ south. It has about 5° 18′ longitude from
east to west. It is generally high mountainous land,
mixed with large valleys, which, as well as the mountains appeared very fertile; and in most places that
we saw, the trees are very large, tall and thick. It
is also very well inhabited with strong well-limbed
negroes, whom we found very daring and bold at

several places. As to the product of it, I know no
more than what I have said in my account of Port
Montague; but it is very probable this island may
afford as many rich commodities as any in the world;
and the natives may be easily brought to commerce,
though I could not pretend to it under my present circumstances.

Being near the island to the northward of the
volcano, I sent my boat to sound, thinking to anchor
here, but she returned and brought me word, that they
had no ground till they met with a reef of coral rocks
about a mile from the shore, then I bore away to the
north side of the island, where we found no anchoring
neither. We saw several people, and some cocoa-nut
trees, but could not send ashore for want of my pinnace,
which was out of order. In the evening I stood off to
sea, to be at such a distance that I might not be driven
by any current upon the shoals of this island, if it
should prove calm. We had but little wind, especially
the beginning of the night; but in the morning I found
myself so far to the west of the island, that the wind
being at east-south-east, I could not fetch it, wherefore
I kept on to the southward, and stemmed with the body
of a high island about eleven or twelve leagues long,
lying to the southward of that which I before designed for. I named this island Sir George Rook's
Island.

We also saw some other islands to the westward,
which may be better seen in my draft of these lands

than here described; but seeing a very small island
lying to the north-west of the long island which was
before us, and not far from it, I steered away for that,
hoping to find anchoring there; and having but little
wind, I sent my boat before to sound, which, when we
were about two miles' distance from the shore, came on
board and brought me word that there was good anchoring in thirty or forty fathom water, a mile from the
isle, and within a reef of the rocks which lay in a half-
moon, reaching from the north part of the island to the
south-east; so at noon we got in and anchored in
thirty-six fathom, a mile from the isle.

In the afternoon I sent my boat ashore to the island,
to see what convenience there was to haul our vessel
ashore in order to be mended, and whether we could
catch any fish. My men in the boat rowed about the
island, but could not land by reason of the rocks and a
great surge running in upon the shore. We found
variation here, 8° 25' west.

I designed to have stayed among these islands till I
got my pinnace refitted; but having no more than one
man who had skill to work upon her, I saw she would
be a long time in repairing (which was one great
reason why I could not prosecute my discoveries further); and the easterly winds being set in, I found I
should scarce be able to hold my ground.

The 31st, in the forenoon, we shot in between two
islands, lying about four leagues asunder, with intention to pass between them. The southernmost is a long

island, with a high hill at each end; this I named
Long Island. The northernmost is a round high island
towering up with several heads or tops, something resembling a crown; this I named Crown Isle from its
form. Both these islands appeared very pleasant, having
spots of green savannahs mixed among the wood-land:
the trees appeared very green and flourishing, and
some of them looked white and full of blossoms. We
passed close by Crown Isle, saw many cocoa-nut trees
on the bays and sides of the hills; and one boat was
coming off from the shore, but returned again. We
saw no smoke on either of the islands, neither did we
see any plantations, and it is probable they are not very
well peopled. We saw many shoals near Crown Island,
and reefs of rocks running off from the points a mile
or more into the sea: my boat was once overboard, with
design to have sent her ashore, but having little wind,
and seeing some shoals, I hoisted her in again, and
stood off out of danger.

In the afternoon, seeing an island bearing north-
west-by-west, we steered away north-west-by-north,
to be to the northward of it. The next morning, being
about midway from the islands we left yesterday, and
having this to the westward of us, the land of the main of
New Guinea within us to the southward, appeared very
high. When we came within four or five leagues of
this island to the west of us, four boats came off to
view us, one came within call, but returned with the
other three without speaking to us; so we kept on for

the island, which I named Sir R. Rich's Island. It was pretty high, woody, and mixed with savannahs like those formerly mentioned. Being to the north of it, we saw an opening between it and another island two leagues to the west of it, which before appeared all in one. The main seemed to be high land, trending to the westward.

On Tuesday, the 2nd of April, about eight in the morning, we discovered a high-peaked island to the westward, which seemed to smoke at its top: the next day we passed by the north side of the Burning Island, and saw smoke again at its top, but the vent lying on the south side of the peak, we could not observe it distinctly, nor see the fire. We afterwards opened three more islands, and some land to the southward, which we could not well tell whether it were islands or part of the main. These islands are all high, full of fair trees and spots of great savannahs, as well the Burning Isle as the rest; but the Burning Isle was more round and peaked at top, very fine land near the sea, and for two-thirds up it: we also saw another isle sending forth a great smoke at once, but it soon vanished, and we saw it no more; we saw also among these islands three small vessels with sails, which the people of Nova Britannia seem wholly ignorant of.

The 11th, at noon, having a very good observation, I found myself to the northward of my reckoning, and thence concluded that we had a current setting north-west, or rather more westerly, as the land lies. From that time to the next morning we had fair clear weather, and a fine moderate gale from south-east to east-by-north: but at daybreak the clouds began to fly, and it lightened very much in the east, south-east, and north-east. At sun-rising, the sky looked very red in the east near the horizon, and there were many black clouds both to the south and north of it. About a quarter of an hour after the sun was up, there was a squall to the windward of us; when on a sudden one of our men on the forecastle called out that he saw something astern, but could not tell what: I looked out for it, and immediately saw a spout beginning to work within a quarter of a mile of us, exactly in the wind: we presently put right before it. It came very swiftly, whirling the water up in a pillar about six or seven yards high. As yet I could not see any pendulous cloud, from whence it might come, and was in hopes it would soon lose its force. In four or five minutes' time it came within a cable's length of us, and passed away to leeward, and then I saw a long pale stream coming down to the whirling water. This stream was about the bigness of a rainbow: the upper end seemed vastly high, not descending from any dark cloud, and therefore the more strange to me, I never having seen the like before. It passed about a mile to leeward of us, and then broke. This was but a small spout, not strong nor lasting; yet I perceived much wind in it as it passed by us. The current still continued at north-west a little westerly, which I allowed to run a mile per hour.

By an observation the 13th, at noon, I found myself 25′ to the northward of my reckoning; whether occasioned by bad steerage, a bad account, or a current, I could not determine; but was apt to judge it might be a complication of all; for I could not think it was wholly the current, the land here lying east-by-south, and west-by-north, or a little more northerly and southerly. We had kept so nigh as to see it, and at farthest had not been above twenty leagues from it, but sometimes much nearer; and it is not probable that any current should set directly off from a land. A tide indeed may; but then the flood has the same force to strike in upon the shore, as the ebb to strike off from it: but a current must have set nearly along shore, either easterly or westerly; and if anything northerly or southerly, it could be but very little in comparison of its east or west course, on a coast lying as this doth; which yet we did not perceive. If therefore we were deceived by a current, it is very probable that the land is here disjoined, and that there is a passage through to the southward, and that the land from King William's Cape to this place is an island, separated from New Guinea by some strait, as Nova Britannia is by that which we came through. But this being at best but a probable conjecture, I shall insist no farther upon it.

The 14th we passed by Scouten's Island, and Providence Island, and found still a very strong current setting to the north-west. On the 17th we saw a high mountain

on the main, that sent forth great quantities of smoke
from its top : this volcano we did not see in our voyage
out.   In the afternoon we discovered **King William's
Island**, and crowded all the sail we could to get near
it before night, thinking to lie to the eastward of it till
day, for fear of some shoals that lie at the west end of
it.   Before night we got within two leagues of it, and
having a fine gale of wind and a light moon, I resolved
to pass through in the night, which I hoped to do before
twelve o'clock, if the gale continued ; but when we
came within two miles of it, it fell calm : yet afterwards
by the help of the current, a small gale, and our boat,
we got through before day.   In the night we had a
very fragrant smell from the island.   By morning
light we were got two leagues to the westward of it ;
and then were becalmed all the morning ; and met
such whirling tides, that when we came into them, the
ship turned quite round : and though sometimes we
had a small gale of wind, yet she could not feel the helm
when she came into these whirlpools : neither could we
get from amongst them, till a brisk gale sprung up ;
yet we drove not much any way, but whirled round
like a top.   And those whirlpools were not constant to
one place but drove about strangely : and sometimes
we saw among them large ripplings of the water, like
great over-falls making a fearful noise.   I sent my
boat to sound, but found no ground.

The 18th Cape Mabo bore south, distance nine leagues ;
by which account it lies in the latitude of 50′ south,

and meridian distance from Cape St. George one thousand two hundred and forty-three miles. St. John's Isle lies forty-eight miles to the east of Cape St. George; which being added to the distance between Cape St. George and Cape Mabo, makes one thousand two hundred and ninety-one meridional parts; which was the furthest that I was to the east. In my outward-bound voyage I made meridian distance between Cape Mabo and Cape St. George, one thousand two hundred and ninety miles; and now in my return, but one thousand two hundred and forty-three; which is forty-seven short of my distance going out. This difference may probably be occasioned by the strong western current which we found in our return, which I allowed for after I perceived it; and though we did not discern any current when we went to the eastward, except when near the islands, yet it is probable we had one against us, though we did not take notice of it because of the strong westerly winds. King William's Island lies in the latitude of 21' south, and may be seen distinctly off Cape Mabo.

In the evening we passed by Cape Mabo; and afterwards steered away south-east half-east, keeping along the shore, which here trends south-easterly. The next morning, seeing a large opening in the land, with an island near the south side; I stood in, thinking to anchor there. When we were shot in within two leagues of the island, the wind came to the west, which blows right into the opening. I stood to the north shore,

intending, when I came pretty nigh, to send my boat
into the opening, and sound, before I would venture in.
We found several deep bays, but no soundings within
two miles of the shore; therefore I stood off again.
then seeing a rippling under our lee, I sent my boat to
sound on it; which returned in half an hour, and
brought me word that the rippling we saw was only a
tide, and that they had no ground there.

Printed by Cassell & Company, Limited, La Belle Sauvage. London, E.C.

30—1092

VOLUMES PUBLISHED in
Cassell's Standard Library.

Price 1s. each; or in cloth, 2s. each.

CASSELL & COMPANY, LIMITED, *Ludgate Hill, London.*

Science and Natural History.

The Story of the Heavens. By Sir ROBERT STAWELL BALL, F.R.S., F.R.A.S. With Coloured Plates and Wood Engravings. *Popular Edition.* 12s. 6d.

Star-Land. Being Talks with Young People about the Wonders of the Heavens. By Sir ROBERT STAWELL BALL. Illustrated. 6s.

Science for All. Edited by Dr. ROBERT BROWN, M.A., F.L.S., &c. Five Volumes. With about 1,500 Illustrations. 9s. each.

Our Earth and its Story. Edited by Dr. ROBERT BROWN, M.A., F.L.S., &c. With 36 Coloured Plates and numerous Wood Engravings. Complete in Three Volumes. 9s. each.

Electricity in the Service of Man. Translated and Edited by R. WORMELL, D.Sc., M.A. With nearly 850 Illustrations. *Cheap Edition.* 9s.

Practical Electricity. By Prof. W. E. AYRTON, F.R.S. Illustrated throughout. 7s. 6d.

Colour. By Prof. A. H. CHURCH. *Enlarged Edition,* with Six Coloured Plates. 3s. 6d.

Beetles, Butterflies, Moths, and other Insects. With 12 Coloured Plates. Cloth, 3s. 6d.

Cassell's New Natural History. Edited by Prof. P. MARTIN DUNCAN, M.B., F.R.S. Complete in Six Volumes. With 2,000 Illustrations. 9s. each.

Cassell's Concise Natural History. By Prof. E. PERCEVAL WRIGHT, M.D. Fully Illustrated. Cloth, 7s. 6d.

Nature's Wonder Workers. Being some Short Life Histories in the Insect World. By KATE R. LOVELL. Illustrated. 3s. 6d.

Familiar Wild Birds. By W. SWAYSLAND, F.Z.S. With Coloured Illustrations. Complete in FOUR SERIES. 12s. 6d. each.

Birds' Nests, Eggs, and Egg-Collecting. By R. KEARTON. With 16 Coloured Plates of Eggs. 5s.

European Butterflies and Moths. With 61 Coloured Plates. Cloth gilt, 35s.

Commercial Botany of the Nineteenth Century. By J. R. JACKSON, A.L.S., of the Royal Gardens, Kew. 3s. 6d.

CASSELL & COMPANY, LIMITED, *Ludgate Hill, London.*

Biography.

The Diplomatic Reminiscences of Lord Augustus
Loftus, P.C., G.C.B., 1837—1862. Two Vols., 32s

Salisbury Parliament, A Diary of the. By H. W.
Lucy. Illustrated by HARRY FURNISS. Cloth gilt, 21s.

The Career of Columbus. By CHARLES ELTON, F.S.A.
With Map. Cloth, 10s. 6d.

Cassell's New Biographical Dictionary, containing
Memoirs of the Most Eminent Men and Women of all Ages and
Countries. 768 pages, demy 8vo, cloth, 7s. 6d.

Vernon Heath's Recollections. 10s. 6d.

Lord Houghton. By T. WEMYSS REID. Two Volumes,
with Two Portraits, 32s.

Watts Phillips, Artist and Playwright. By Miss
E. WATTS PHILLIPS. With 32 Plates. Royal 8vo. 10s. 6d.

Richard Redgrave, C.B., R.A. Illustrated. 10s. 6d.

Shaftesbury, The Life and Work of the Seventh
Earl of. By EDWIN HODDER. *Cheap Edition.* 3s. 6d.

The Journal of Marie Bashkirtseff. 7s. 6d.

The Letters of Marie Bashkirtseff. 7s. 6d.

The Life of the Rev. J. G. Wood. By his Son, the
Rev. THEODORE WOOD. With Portrait. *Cheap Edition.* 5s.

Father Mathew : His Life and Times. By FRANK
J. MATHEW, a Grand-Nephew. 2s. 6d.

Topography.

Africa and its Explorers, The Story of. By Dr.
ROBERT BROWN, M.A., &c. Illustrated. Vol. I. 7s. 6d.

Historic Houses of the United Kingdom. Pro-
fusely Illustrated. Complete in One Vol., cloth gilt, 10s. 6d.

Our Own Country. With about 1,200 Original Illustrations. Complete in Six Vols., cloth, 7s. 6d. each. *Library Edition,*
Three Double Vols., £1 17s. 6d. the set.

Old and New Edinburgh, Cassell's. Complete in
Three Volumes, with 600 Illustrations. Extra crown 4to, cloth, 9s. each ;
or in Library binding, Three Vols., £1 10s.

The Countries of the World. By Dr. ROBERT BROWN,
F.R.G.S. With about 750 Illustrations. Complete in Six Vols., cloth,
7s. 6d. each ; or Three Vols., Library binding, 37s. 6d.

Cities of the World. Illustrated throughout. Four Vols.,
7s. 6d. each.

Old and New London. Complete in Six Volumes, with
about 1,200 Engravings, 9s. each. *Library Edition,* imitation rox-
burgh, £3. Vols. I. and II. are by WALTER THORNBURY, the other
Vols. are by EDWARD WALFORD.

Greater London. By EDWARD WALFORD. With about
400 Original Illustrations. Two Vols., 9s. each. *Library Edition,*
Two Vols., £1.

CASSELL & COMPANY, LIMITED, *Ludgate Hill, London.*

www.ingramcontent.com/pod-product-compliance
Lightning Source LLC
Chambersburg PA
CBHW030550040726
47497CB00008B/2653